The Evangel

of

Calico

CHARLES E. MILLER

Order this book online at www.trafford.com
or email orders@trafford.com

Most Trafford titles are also available at major online book retailers.

Printed in the United States of America.

ISBN: 978-1-4669-9958-9 (sc)
ISBN: 978-1-4669-9959-6 (hc)
ISBN: 978-1-4669-9960-2 (e)

Library of Congress Control Number: 2013910648

Trafford rev. 06/06/2013

   www.trafford.com

North America & international
toll-free: 1 888 232 4444 (USA & Canada)
fax: 812 355 4082

*T*he cables rattled against each other as the platform settled down into the hole as the total darkness closed in about Duval. He was alone on the deck. His visit to the mine was a courtesy call and authorized by the owner, a man named Clyde Gibson, whose residence was not in Calico but in San Francisco. Duval's boss, newspaper editor of the *Eagle*, Mr. Dixon, had arranged for the reporter's visit. The chill of the deep mine shaft surrounded the awaited arrival of the supervisor's chamber, off the main elevator shaft. It gave Duval some relief to see the kerosene lantern flames, sharp against the blotto blackness of the darkness of the chamber opening. The platform, called the lift, settled into position before the cavern of supervisor McCloud.

Duval lifted the gate latch and stepped into the chamber of McCloud.

"You again, the newspaper reporter!"

"I'm here to observe and write a report for my paper, sir. Folks in Calico know about the silver mine. I want to give them the picture."

"Of the sweaty bodies of twenty men hacking away at the mountain with picks and shovels?"

"That's right, sir. It's their mountain." The supervisor answered this comment with a skeptical grunt and turned to pick a numbered brass badge from a board for the reporter to wear on his tour below.

"I could have guessed. I wanted to see for myself." Duval pinned the number badge to his shirt. "I won't interfere. I'll do as ordered," Duval reassured McCloud.

"Here. Yer gonna need some light down there." The supervisor plucked a helmet from a peg and clamped a burning lantern onto the miner's helmet.

"Keep this with you at all times. Lose this light, Mr. Reporter, and it's one way to lose your way in the mine. Get it?"

"Yes, sir."

"It's one thing to lose your way in a mine tunnel, and it's another to be buried behind tons of mountain fall in."

"I hear you, sir." Duval put on the helmet.

"Turn in the tag and helmet in when yer done. Don't go and leave either of 'em down in the pit."

Duval turned and walked back onto the platform, clanging the gauge behind him. McCloud rang a brass gong one time, and the platform slowly descended into the darkness of the shaft.

It required only minutes for the platform to settle with a thump. Duval saw what he expected. The miners, about twenty of them, were working on the rock faces of the tunnel, boring into the mountain with the hard metallic clank of their shovels and metallic spit of the pick ends. There was no conversation between them; their arduous labor made the distress of necessary conversation the cloak of their labor. Many of them had removed their shirts. Their tawny and white skins glistened with drops of sweat in the light from their helmet lanterns. The looms from their helmet lanterns flashed, crisscrossed, and scrambled in weird shapes and dimensions, at once giving illumination to the chamber.

"Grant, Harvey, comeeres." The two men—one with a pick and the other a shovel—ran to where the boss and Duval stood.

"Start diggin' a hole under that drip." He shone his lantern up at the ceiling where the drip continued every two seconds. Rock must be porous. Porous . . . water can settle as fast as it drips, like nature. Within minutes, the two miners had dug a pit directly beneath the ceiling drip. "If the bowl empties before it can fill, hell, we oughtn't stay 'round here, sand in the rocks, water, could burst! I make a report of this. I call the owner and consult with the super. If they say so, we abandon this here tunnel. We gotta keep an eye on the water drip, so we know jes where we stan'. If that there pothole fills, then we bring down a pump to suck the water up to the surface. We got no other choice, lest we want to abandon the this tunnel entirely. That wouldn't be much help so far's mining silver goes."

While this activity was going on, Duval scribbled a note in the form of single word into his notepad. "Pack rats, water drip pumps." He began to feel the chill of the mine.

"Le's hope all goes well. If not, by gawd I'll sound the alarm." By this time, the other miners had stopped work and are watching the pit boss, Duval, the two miners who had dug the pot hole . . . to see what they were up to. Instinctively, they feared such a conference on the job and feared, most of all, not being told what, if anything adverse, was going on. They sensed the water danger; some of the men had followed the lantern of the pit boss when he shined on the cling rock where, to this moment, the drip continued without abatement.

"Well, if an unsafe condition breaks out, we leave the line until I can arrange some changes. The inspector can determine fer himself if it's safe for the miners to return."

At the end of the tunnel, dug deeper and deeper into the mountain, Duval saw a miner with a hose spraying the floor where half a dozen men were digging.

"You hose down the dust. You got that right, Mr. Duval." So much dust. Breathing in the dust and they die from not being able to breathe. "Good idea," Duval remarked offhand.

"Thets his job . . . to keep hacking and working on the mountain, Mr. Duval, and to keep the dust damp and settled," said the pit boss. He scanned the rocks of the tunnel ceiling again and saw that the drip of the water had not increased. "It could be a river jes above that there drip, Duval. Lyke you'd be a casualty like the rest of us."

"I don't plan to."

"Nothing that ever happens down here . . . except the digging and shoveling . . . is ever counted on. Now you know two dangers . . . and them rats can take over the pit if there's enough of 'em. Methane . . . sometimes. It ain't like coal mining where the coal is formed by decay over centuries. This here's a different kind a rock . . . performed by heat. But hear me, Duval, There's chasms, ridges, breaks in the rock caused by earthquakes. Y' can see eternity. So down you go wanderin' 'round any, y hear?"

"I hear y', Mr. Smith."

"We actual lost a man six months ago . . . stepped off into space and was gone. We couldn't hear him after a while down into the crack. Like a crevice in the ice, it were so deep, we couldn't reach him, passed down some food . . . he stopped hollerin' after a while, sleeping or dead."

Lighting, with here and there sparkles of residual silver, buried in rock faces the miners worked. It was a scene possessing a strange mystique of timeless labor and uncertain results. Half of the miners had removed their shirts, kept their helmets on their heads, the kerosene lamps giving focus to their work.

The steely sound of the iron picks against the stone bit the cool air constantly in a broken staccato accompanied by the gravely scrape of the shovels as other miners loaded the six ore cars that stood idle on the track. The entire process of extracting the silver ore appeared mechanical, as if these men were somehow working off their penalties for their sins damned for an eternity to this labor.

"I'm Jake Smi," sounded a surly voice behind Duval. He turned to face the pit boss standing behind him. "What brings you back again, Duval?" The pit boss remembered his name. "Same thing . . . . a story. Readers want to know more. We got a lot of city folks read my paper."

"Not much to it. This here work, I mean. Jes dig and shovel, dig and shovel."

Duval said nothing. He watched the men laboring in the pit, sometimes called the tunnel. Duval marveled that there was no exchange of words . . . only the sounds of the miners' tools working on the hard rock filled the air. The beams from the miners' lanterns flashed from off smooth rock surfaces. Pieces of blue turquoise flashed now and then like jewels hidden in the rock.

"What you see is what you get," said the pit boss.

"Danger." He heard a bark. "You've got a dog down here!" Duval exclaimed.

"Got to. It's a rat catcher."

"Rats, down here!"

"They're sometimes big enough to drag a man's lunch box out of sight. Pack rats. They come from nowhere. We keep a dog to bark them . . . scared, they run. Every once in a while, a miner catch one and smashes it with his pick or the back of his shovel."

"Why are they way down here?"

"Food. They can scamper through layers of rock . . . nobody knows how . . . a mile from the surface. The critters can smell man food fer a mile. And strong. You wouldn't believe it, but I seen a pack rat drag a miner's lunch off to a distance."

"Scavengers. Maybe they catch a ride on the ore carts . . . or in the elevator. They can even come down on the cables . . . like boarding a ship by the mooring ropes."

"We keep that dawg jes so they don' come and bother us none. Every now and then, Savage—thet's the dawg's name—eer now and then, he catches one in his teeth and kills it. We bury it under the rock. When them rats smells food . . . look out!" Duval kept silent as he watched the lights flicker, clash, beam, and vanish into total dark. Suddenly the pit boss looked upward.

"Oh, damn, damn, damn!" He flashed a kerosene lantern with a lens up to the ceiling of the tunnel. He fixed the light on a dripping of water from a rock. Duval looked upward.

"Of all things tha' kin happen, we break into a underground river . . . too deep fer a water table. Then God help us! We're done fer. Water can fill the tunnel . . . like a flood, by god so fast we drown like them rats." Duval looked upward and watched the steady dripping from the ceiling rock.

"That's about it . . . the danger, I mean."

"Oh, no . . . pockets of methane once in a while . . . old stuff, but it's there."

"What about explosions?" Duval asked.

"We got a good man handle that. 'Casionally amber breaks loose. Gotta watch all the time for such things. If y' hear 'fire in the hole,' hit the groun', Duval, the blast of thet there TNT will knock ye into hell and come back."

"I saw it first time I was here."

"Don' niver . . . don' niver count on nothin' happenin'. I mean, naturally nature plays tricks on la man."

"Timber!" came a cry.

"We've got a new load of beams. We've got to put up shoring as we go along. See there. The miners began to erect the shoring at every ten yards of tunnel that lacked any support from the twelve-by-twelve log beams and the ten-by-ten cross beams."

"We got our ways. We know what were adoin'."

"Those jewels, the blue stone . . . turquoise, I think they're called, how do you save them?"

"At the crusher . . . we pick them out . . . helps pay for the operation, sells on the market for jewels," said the pit boss.

"They're taken out when the ore is crushed."

"Extracting silver is the big job . . . now they think on . . . 'lectrolysis, putting the ore into a pit and making the 'lectricity take the silver from the rocks. Some say acid is better. They be atrying different ways to 'xtract the silver."

At about that moment in the words of the pit boss's explanation of the process of extraction, a chunk of rock fell to the floor. The pit boss pushed Duval to one side where they stood and scanned the ceiling with his lantern. By good fortune, no miner was hit by the rock fall.

"See what I mean about nature? The hazards of hell, Duval. You gotta believe it."

Tricklings of loose sand fell on the backs of the miners where they stood, watching the ceiling for that fatal collapse that could and would entomb them. Their bare bodies and shirts were coated in sweat. Occasionally a miner would stop for a drink from his canteen cup, the water dipped from a barrel.

Without warning, there came an enormous cracking sound. All the miners at once dropped their tools and, running toward the ore carts, crouched down beside them. Duval got down. A huge cracking of tortured stone and the rumble of the earth carried a wall of debris at the end of the tunnel that advanced fifteen yards, covering the tools and the work that had been going on. The pit boss bore a look of desperate fear on his face at the ceiling as he threw his light into the rock above their heads and at the walls, waiting for the the cracking sound of splitting heavy wood timbers; but after several minutes, with small rock falls that showed the instability of the formation, the shaking ceased.

"Gotta know the warning sounds and signs. That dripping of water was a giveaway that something was going on above us.

God's grace.

Duval said nothing. They waited for a following tremor, but none came.

"All right, men, do yer best, clear the rocks and continue the tunnel. Any wants to leave the mine kin do so. Dock yer pay." There came no response from the miners.

They work for their living and face the look of death. "Put that linter yer paper."

Smith threw his light up to the ceiling again where the dripping had occurred, but now the dripping had increased.

"All right men, load up! We gotta git outa here . . . load up on that platform! There's something about to happen."

The miners grabbed their shirts—those not buried in the rock fall. They walked toward the cars and dropped their tools into the carts and the platform beyond. They then loaded onto the platform, no talk amongst them, as they stood in the silence of impending death and fear on their faces.

"All y', when and if it's safe to return, I'll letcha know. Okay? This here mine's a rich one, owner won't give it up. We'll stat digging another direction."

The miners and Duval, now loaded, awaited the clang of the bell that signaled the rise to the surface of the earth, stopping first at the supervisor's cove to turn in their badges . . . those not lost in the rock fall. The gong rang, and the platform began to rise up out of the darkness of a dangerous condition in the mine.

"Put this into yer paper. They miners quit early today. A slight shake up changed the . . . the gen'l looks of the mine . . . down un'erground. Shaft. We'll be mining fer silver when it's safe to do so."

When the miners' elevator reached the supervisor's chamber, each man—those whose shirts were not buried— removed his badge and took off his helmet, extinguishing the light of his lamp. He placed these items in the regulation places along one wall in the chamber. Their chore completed and the men accounted for, loading up, the platform rose to the surface. Duval was relieved to see the dusk light and to know that he would not have to walk back to his hotel in the darkness. Tonight was the night he was to show up for dinner at his editor's house. He had no time to waste. The miners walked away in conversation and mute silence, still agitated by the gravity of their ordeal down in the mine. The pit boss and supervisor had their reports to make, as did Duval for the paper. There was too much to tell.

At his hotel, Duval greeted the clerk. He clumped with fatigue up to his room, attempting some sort of cleaning for his visit to his boss's house. They would have to understand what he had gone through and the conditions of a visit to the Empire Mine.

$\mathcal{T}$he tall head frame rose forty feet on the hillside, above the town of Calico. The structure was fresh wood, gleamed amber in the morning light, the pit into which the lift would dop had just begun to the first level. Below the mountainside, a cluster of five cabins gave evidence of human occupation of the small valley. Two miners, one named Clemens and the other Rick, had discovered silver in the streambed that fed from out of the nearby mountains. The miners had formed a camp. They were certain, all eight of them, that there were quantities of silver in the hills. They were determined to stay. Already they had staked out claims along the nearby stream that fed down the main road into the town. Named for the shirt that Rick wore, fashioned by his wife back in Missouri, Calico became the name for this early mining town. Clemens had discovered the shine of silver amid the rocks in the stream; Rock had confirmed the find. Together, they staked their claim of one hundred yards on both sides of the stream they named Turquoise, for it had become evident that turquoise, pure blue and saleable in San Francisco for jewelry and ornamentation of many ores, was a by-product of their silver diggings. They knew they had much work to do.

Calico remained quiet and unnoticed, off the main highway west of the hamlet. Another small town named Lee Vining having sprung up to accommodate travelers. It was a stagecoach stop for the Butterfield line. Calico, which lay some four miles to the east, was more of a courtesy run, depending on the driver of the stage and the urgency of his passengers.

The pioneers of this old silver town, now a new spike in the landscape, was their relation that to build a town on any side they would need great quantities of wood. The nearest sawmill was to the south approaching Visalia. Then there was a sawmill up toward the small towns of Tahoe. They would have to ship their timber in if they wanted to construct houses and business buildings and the like. Rick called together five of the settlers in Calico and proposed that they purchase the necessary equipment to start a sawmill of their own. They could arrange to have logs of a practical size waggoned in from the woods to the north, up near the Trinity River. Then it was settled. And the more aggressive businessman of the two prospectors went to the town of Creon and arranged for the machinery. Within three months, the two prospectors, with the help of the other settlers, had their own sawmill working; and thus timber for the growth of the town now had its source in the Clemns-Rick sawmill of Calico. They dredged a pond with the help of a mile and a wooden plow as a pond for the incoming logs. Two of the settlers had carpenter experience. It was one of the anomalies of these early western towns that any man with the slightest experience, whether in plowing, sawing of logs, dragging logs by mule and chain, rock work, and the driving of pegs was in demand. The benefactors of this initial labor did not inquire as to working background . . . just that they had the rare yet necessary talent to use in construction.

The town grew. The wooden head frame turned gray yet was as solid and dependable as the first day the laborers erected it in the mining site. The main shaft continued to go down. More miners, having heard by stagecoach that there were opportunities in Calico, drifted into the town and soon found work for their hands and imaginations.

The main street, which some called Bastard Street, too shape, board sidewalks on one side fronted a tavern, a candle iers, a gunsmith. Down the street, Smithy had set up his forge and anvil and the metallic clink could be heard on many days in the cold, the air of the Sierra foothills community. People, men mostly, gravitated into Calico from all parts of the country. Within the space of five years and a meager output from the Empire Silver Mine, so-called because Rick envisioned himself a rich man in a poor man's dungarees, the town grew and it prospered. Miniscule amounts of silver dust made their way into San Francisco. The process was painful, a far thrust from later engines of production. Within the next year, year six in Calico, Rick purchased the first stamping mill. Rock wheeled down from the mine shaft was thrust under the powerful pistons of the stamping mill and, having been crushed, was subjected to an acid bath that leeched out the silver to the bottom of the trays; the rock debris was flushed away into what became in tie, reat piles of silver ore slag. There was about this entire process, from the pick and shovel work down in the deepening shaft and the second spur tunnel, a certain breathless expectation of wealth to come. This was no mere quest for a worthless product. Wislve on the market, especially silver leeched from ore rather than low-grade silver ore, had a commercial value that would sustain the inhabitants of Calico for many decades, providing the town lived and providing the silver deposits under the mountain did not run out.

One woman entered Calico as the wife of a businessman who, enlightened by stories of the Far West and thrilled by the thought that he too could become a pioneer and with all—if its lustrous and energetic meaning, its expansive vision of the weirdness . . . and this area in the Sierra Foothills was, indeed, a wilderness at this time—could share into the prospect of wealth in the ground and, in fact, on top of the ground when the town became a logging community. And so Kate, that was her name, migrated to Calico with her husband who, with soft white hands unaccustomed to physical labor, soon became adapted to the hard conditions of pioneer community living. He learned how to show a horse along Bastard Street. He learned how to mend harness, became a leather worker of sorts, the appellative attached to anyone who was learning a new trade, a carpenter of sorts, a wagoneer of sorts. But there was no disdain in the words, only an acknowledgement that the newcomers were putting in their apprenticeship at a new trade. In a short time, as the town continued to attract settlers, they would become wealthy in their owns right by the labor of their hands and the dedication of their minds and spirits. The settlement in Calico was a challenge to the human spirit, a thing ennobling in a way, and certainly a trial for the man's will, his physical strength and his willingness to endure amid risks and failures. The early people in Calico considered themselves to be pioneers, and as they most certainly are, they undertook strange tasks, unusual challenges, dangerous risks, and energetic enterprises with a certain spirit of daring and joy.

A wagoneer erected his own building; a pioneer investor in properties had a small two-storey hotel erected across from an auditorium, so it was called, that became a dance hall for wild Saturday night reverie. Clement and Rick tried to instill the notion that a town could not simply sprawl. There had to be signed streets for visitors and newcomers, and so it came about. A son of one of the miners who worked in the Empire Mine painted some street signs, and with his papa's great pride, he erected them at strategic corners in the township of Calico. Nobody knew where to apply for a license to open a shop, in which street. Common sense usually determined the location of new stores—a dry goods store, a gunsmith's place, a general store, a bank, the doctor's house . . . oh, yes, a Doctor Holmes had migrated to Calico, partly to assuage his asthma in the clear mountain air, but also to practice medicine in a community that would increasingly need to call upon his care and attention. Injuries were a common reminder of the nature of the town's basic mission, to mine silver. Here and there a disease was introduced—an outside who had come to Calico to recover from bronchitis, epilepsy, diseases of the stomach, pancreas and liver . . . too much alcohol in the big city of San Francisco. They came for these personal reasons. They also came for the adventure, being perhaps the last floodtide of pioneer immigrants from heavily populated cities to the actual wilderness. For, before they of silver, what had the small valley below the Sierras been, what if not a wilderness open to the need, work, wonder and thrill, and hardship of newcomers form cities across the country. Within ten years of their finding of silver, the towns had grown to a population of five hundred souls. The pounding of now a second stamping mill could be heard throughout the night, the machinery fed by water power from the one incidental creek in which Rick had first discovered the presence of silver.

Five hundred and among them women, wives, mothers, and their children. Clemens, always an opportunity in finding labor to do the job, hired all the boys he could muster to dig three wells along Bastard Street. He appointed a miner to oversee the work. It took well over a year for the wells to go into the ground, along a shrewdly plotted groundwater reservoir that a newcomer, an engineer, had pointed out to Rick one day over a beer at the Shallows Tavern. And from the fire wells came line existence, buckets waggoned from San Francisco hung on pegs, it hats of gin . . . not much more. The shrewd management of Clements had brought into existence a cadre of firefighting townsmen, the well-digging boys being appointed to serve as water boys in the event of a failure. Twenty bucks painted red were evident. It is to the credit and basic honesty of the pioneers that the buckets remained on their pegs and were not stolen.

As the towns grew in population, it became a stopping point for vendors, dry goods salesmen on the road, vendors of Hürlimann beer and French wine, purveyors, and vendors of dry goods, apparel for both men and women. Farmers from the mideast had migrated to Calico as the word spread like a whispered well-kept secret. One man, named Doakes, John Doakes, was a farmer, a husbandman, and a butcher. He had wagoned into Calico with a small herd of beef cattle, which he kept over a rise in the hill, east of the town. He was about to supply Calico with some beef, later pork, much to the delight of the townsfolk. A number of the people tried to raise vegetables for their tables and or sale at the open air market, a new thing on one of the side streets and very popular with the townsfolk.

Smithy Peter Locke fabricated shovel, pikes, mining tools, pry bars, spades, chains for the use in the Empire Mine. He oversaw the construction of a rail, rundowns from the mind to the stamping mills, which by this time had ytwn pistons crushing the silver ore. Inside the galvanized shed, the first of its kind, Clemens had had constructed a huge bowl of pottery that contained muriatic acid used to leech the silver from the crushed ore. All these changes, innovations, crudely engineered improvements added to the wealth of Calico so that it began to shine in the sun, so to speak. Here and there, a settler had shingled his roof, but mostly they were covered with galvanized tin imported for San Francisco. What the settlers could not import they made a valiant effort to fabricate. They were producers of a reminent sort, perhaps the only sort in the world. Of course, the Swees had brought their log cabin knowledge to America when they settled along the Hudson River, and the Germans had imported their engineering science of sleighs and measures for hay-hauling logs, boulders, timbers. But because Calico lay out of the reach of common commerce and land navigation, its wilderness character inspired the settlers to invent, exploit, improvise, and construct. They were builders of the first character.

Prospectors for silver came into Calico, at first by the dozens, or so it appeared, from cities and towns in the east seeking wealth and eminence. Many of them left when they realized that the silver to be mined in any great quantity came from the tunnels into Empire Mountain. They were not shrewd enough to encamp by the creek and try their luck for a month or two. Silver prospecting had seemed all so simple and easy for the tyro. Preferring their soft lives in the east, they pulled up stakes, literally in some instances, and departed on the next stagecoach out of Calico. The residual residents were the hardy ones, and the fact that they remained in the burgeoning town for at least a year was testimony to their hardiness and their imaginations and their pioneer spirit.

$\mathcal{T}$he Hickory Spur Stagecoach rolled into Calico one Saturday noon from which there disembarked a mother with her little boy and a tall, rangy man with a valise in one hand and a shotgun in the other. His name was Garvey, Garvey Whitlock. He had read about the town in his local paper and the ad placed there by the so-called mayor of the silver town to attract both visitors and permanent residents. Gar had heard that the town was a wild and shooting-up place, alive with bootleggers, bandits, card sharks, and thieves. He wanted any who saw him disengage himself from the Hickory stage to be aware that he was fully capable of protecting himself with a twelve-gauge shotgun. His valise contained a few personal duds and some papers that established his profession as a working journalist. He expected to find work with a newspaper in Calico, if there was one, and if not to start one. Every town, and especially small burgeoning towns like Calico, needed to keep current in the goings-on in the town, not just for information but for their own safety. Garvey checked in at the Graystone Inn, down the boardwalk from the stage stop. He introduced himself to the clerk at the counter. He shoved a gold piece across the counter for a week's room rent and, with scarcely a word, was told that room 4 on the second floor was vacant.

"If you need anything, stranger, jes let me know . . . more towels . . . linen is clean, room swept . . . man died there first week, shot to death. But you got no fear here in Graystone, stranger." The clerk pulled a revolver room under the country. "We try to take care of things 'fore they get really started," he said.

"Cafe . . . restaurant?" Garvey asked.

"Jes down Bastard Street. Oh, excuse me, Miner Street, main hovel here in town, called the Chippendale . . . funny name . . . perty high tones for this town."

"Good. Food's the main thing," said Garvey.

"No women 'lowed in the rooms 'less it's yer wife," said the clerk.

"I'm single and I came here to rest nights, not play games."

"Gotcha," said the clerk. "You'll do."

He said this as if it were a final endorsement of his new tenant in room 4. Garvey took his big latchkey and mounted the steps to his room, around the upper bannister to the front of the building. He would have a room overlooking the main street in Calico.

$\mathcal{T}$he night passed with the stillness of the mountains. Garvey arose early, dressed, washed his face at the basin, pouring water from a pewter pitcher and snatching a hand towel from a rack. His breakfast this morning consisted of a hard bun, a slice of cheese, and water from the same pitcher. His first task was to locate the town newspaper, wherever it was. Surely Calico had a newspaper. Downstairs, at the front desk, he was surprised to find the little man on duty so early. His first impression had been that the clerk was sitting on a stool. In reality he was dangerously short. Garvey asked about mail. He had forgotten to note that this was his first day. The little man reached up with a pair of chef's pincers, scanned a top box, and reported with a shrug. Garvel has an inexplicable sensitivity for the weaknesses in other men. The clerk's was an inherent unwillingness to engage in idle talk. Garvey passed out though the lobby of the Avalanche Hotel and onto the street of his new identity as a citizen of Calico. A boy was raking leaves from the fire gutter, as it was called, silence. Fire buckets had their source in high emergencies in the fire gutter. A well-dressed man had came by in, his gig, drawn by a small mare of iron ray. He could be the doctor, Garvey thought. He walked on up the street, saw the shopkeeper sweeping his boardwalk of a light snowfall in the night, the leather maker, harness and boot leather, actually. He did not glance at Garvey. On up the street, the night's sifting flight snow quickly vanishing from the features of the street. After about three blocks and feeling rather hungry, he stopped at a stand where the native chef was brewing potatoes for sale to passersby, with butter and relish, and a morning nod and a few words. Garvey stopped and purchased a black potato with hot butter, cached in a large napkin. He stopped to taste his breakfast, watching the street life with keen interest. He observed that neither women nor children were to be seen. Perhaps the town was too primitive. A primitive western town, except for a wife willing to face the dangers of a wilderness community did not accompany her husband. Occasionally a doughty younger woman with a penchant for excitement and adventure would travel to a town like Calico to drench herself in whatever life the town had to offer.

Garvey was about to quit his search for a newspaper when he spied a sign that read

"Bureau of Mayhem, town's gazette, the *Eagle*."
This looked like the place. Any name that had wings
on it was a good prospect for a newspaper, even if it
was the *Penguin*.

The grubby little space . . . in such limitless outback . . .
was astonishing to Garvey. He came with pencils, a writing
tablet, a penchant for sketching a scene. He found a square-
shouldered man, a refugee from a logging camp, just tidying
up the small office space with one desk, some cartons in a
corner for cabinet, and a fire bell. The editor—and Garvey
assumed that the man was, in fact, the editor, of the *Eagle*—
smiled at him and greeted him, settling his broom aside. He
walked out of the dust with an outstretched hand.

"Name's Buck. Left the logging trade from a broken
foot . . . and here I am. What's yer business, sir?"

"I'm here to write for your newspaper . . . the *Eagle*, I
expect the name is."

"It is, it is. Sit down, sit down. Smoke."

"Too early in the day . . . but I'll take one for
noontime.

"Just so, just so," the man repeated. "This here's the
Eagle. We publish a newspaper. I heard of a newspaper. It
furnishes the news of the town.

"I wrote for one in 'Frisco, sir."

"Oh, then you got the smarts, all right." The man
continued with his sweeping. It seemed to Garvey that the
fellow was trying to burnish the thick, splintery wooden
floor with his broom.

"So yer here to write for the *Eagle*."

"That's what I said, I'm a writer." He prodded his pad. "I can sketch a little also," said Garvey with a smile, gritting his teeth. He hated self-revelations, but this was employment.

"Well then, take two, meaning the cigars in a vase. Made by a hermit in the mountains, grows his own tobacco, says he's from Appalachia, knows the tricks of the trade."

"There must be a good story or two worth gathering in this here village," said Garvey, noting the man's weakness to reveal the character and content of his newspaper . . . a little deception.

"I see what I see, sir. News has got to be dug out. Usually that's the way it is."

"You got the right hang on that one," said the editor, who by this time had donned a coat that said across the back EDITOR. I got me one friend . . . a soldier from the war, a odd, a old feller who collects news at the gambling hall down the street. You been there"

"WHAT? TO THE GAMBLING HALL."

"Yes."

"Nope. You think I might just find a bit of news there."

"Look, mister, wherever you poke yer head or lift yer hand, there's got to be a news story. Even the old addle men, once a politician in the big city, has got a story as to why he come here to Calico. How's that fer starters."

"Where do I find this . . . retired politician?"

"Same place ye fine other derelicts." said the editor of the *Eagle*.

"Well, now, I'll just jot that down." He removed his tablet a second time and jotted down Gaing House . . . politicians . . . motives.

"Folks who come here to Calico don't always come for silver."

"Silver."

"Yep. Town was founded on silver, mines up on the hill. They take out ten million in silver last year. The Empire Mine. Nothing but a hole in the ground. There's a story there. But yer taking her life in your hands to visit that mine. Had three accidents there last year, two fellers killed."

"Don't say."

"Do say."

"Well now, that gives me two stories, the retired politician. They don't never retire, they jes quit . . . and the mining accident story."

"Explosion. Methane?"

"Methane . . . oh, gas? I heard it sometimes collects in mines."

"Yeah, heard right, stranger. Say . . . what is yer name anyhow?"

"Garvey, Garvey Pawnmaker."

"Well now, there's a business, pawn show. Folks here in Calico don't have too much to own but their good names. But it's a possibility."

"It's a little too early for the gaming house, but the mine. I jes thin I'll go there and address myself."

"One precaution, Mister . . . Mister . . ."

"Pawnmaker."

"Mr. Pawnmaker. Take a light for eye go on into the shafe . . . and they may jes furnish ye with a metal hat, a helmit . . . case a rock breaks loose. You don't want to be killed the first week ye been in Calicos Empire Mine."

"No, that wouldn't be fair to me . . . er to yer paper. I could be your best asset. At this point I don't see any employees hustling out."

"We hating to none. We hire by instinct, by choice, and by necessity, that is."

"Economical, to say the least."

The editor ignored this rejoinder and set about adjusting a small pile of papers. "You wouldn't care to see last month's record, now would ye?"

"Right away, thanks, Mister . . . I don't know yer name."

"Editsoron, like the inventor of the lightbulb. Edison. I got me own lights."

Garvey knew the man's weakness was his hidden pride, but then again, there was no venue for displays of pride in this pioneer village of Calico, not the show of enterprise. He shook Mr. Edisons hand, took a paper from the pile, and left the editorial office of the *Eagle*.

"Mister!" He heard a shout from behind. He turned. "You forgot yer potato. Dongs 'round here don't much like potatoes, lest they got red meat mixed with 'em."

"Oh, shanks. Breakfast, Spartan diet, ye know," said Garvey.

"Good way to start, sir. Take care and good luck. Write her story if ye find one. I'll be interested to read it." Garvey left the *Eagle* office, with a bite into his cooling potato with butter.

*A*bout the editor, Mr. Edison, there is a detail of the man's character that bears strongly on his integrity for communication of the news in Calico, not just his occasional lapse in memory whenever it seemed convenient for him to sustain this slight malady. His capacity for fabricating news by reinventing the incident by giving its importance either a twist of fabrication, in short a lie that misaligns the incident with the truth. Or he will align with the incident an event that bears no particular relevance to the reported event. These two lapses in editorial integrity will in short time gain for him the reputation of a profound and imaginative reporter and bearer of news in Calico, while at the same time alienating those who, being closer to the incidents or the event, have a more, let us say, accurate understanding of what did actually occur. This weakness, this lapse in integrity, will make for Mr. Edison, editor of the *Eagle*, a rapid reputation for reportage, for embellishing the truth slightly and, with that, for bringing to the 'em illiterate population of the village the "unvarnished truth" of great reporting. Garvey would soon discover these lapses in integrity by the way the editor would skew history to conform to his predelections for good news, good reporting, and enlightenment. As for Garvey.

He hiked up the trail to the mine on the mountainside. He stood sketching the timbers, the crude machinery, and the surrounding disposal of the slag. If the paper could reproduce this scene, it would enlighten the world of journalism for certain, Garvey reflected. He checked his watch. He had no idea and had forgotten to inquire about the times for the shifts, when the next elevator loaded with miners would arrive at the surface. As he stood there on the mountainside, he was aware of his height, looking down to the town, actually village, at this time like Calico's history. Six feet two inches, slim and wiry, blue eyes, his billed cap giving to him the aspect of an official observer. He sketched away to picture the mine's head frame, seeing miners by twos and threes, and singly advancing up to the mine along well-beaten trails. The sun threw a canopy of pale yellow light over the ridge, above him the crest of Empire Mine Mountain. He put his pencil and sketch pad away and continued up trail to the mine. The miners greeted one another by their first names. One was smoking a cigar, another chewing on a cud of tobacco. They were men in their thirties and forties, strong yet and uncontaminated by mined us, an affliction common to all hard rock miners, whether for coal or silver or gold. As they approached the shadows of the head frame, cheery hails came from the platform inside the immense log posts of the frame. The miners entered the safety ate. Garvey did likewise, crowding in against some twenty of the crew for this shift. The air was frosty, the light a gloomy collection of gathering shadows. The crew foreman looked at his watch. The men on the platform waited, another five minutes. The foreman pulled a cord. A brass bell below the platform, in what the miners commonly referred to as the hole, signaled the lift operator to commence the descent. Slowly and with some vibration and perceptible movement, the platform began its roll into the hole. The miners stood silent. They wore their metal helmets; the kerosene lanterns were awaiting each man. After about five minutes, during which time the blackness shrouded the lift, the platform came to a stop. A trickle of dust and a small handful of stones fell from above. All eyes turned upward; there was nothing to observe. The ground was alive, a living monster that had been beaten into submission for the purpose of extracting silver ore.

Opposite the lift shone a small chamber lit by kerosene lanters, two from the icing, one at a desk and numbers board. The light was shadowy, special, and mysterious. Facial features and expressions were somber in the shining shadows of light as the men, according to custom, walked past a board on which stood a lantern for each, burning and ready for its installation on the helmet of each miner. Walking past the row of burning lamps, the miners searched for his number and stuck it by a pin into his pocket. Its absence from the board meant that that miner was at work, in the hold, at the bottom of the shaft. All of this activity was performed in virtual silence shaded by hidden fear, an anxiety every miner knows when he goes into the depths of the mountain. Would this day mark his day for burial within the mine by some accident. Powder was set to carve immense chunks If from the walls. Perhaps the line man would make a mistake. Or then again, by merely cutting into the heart of the mountain, a pick could open up a hidden vein of water that within minutes could flood the mine and drown all the men. These were two omnipresent possibilities. An earthquake, rarely, a schism between rock surfaces that slipped before timbers could be brought on to support the fall. There were always one, possibly two stacks of eight by eight timbers for reinforcing the chamber where the miners dug.

On the elevator platform, the supervisor rang the bell, and the lift began its real descent into the hole, a distance of at least one thousand feet. Then later on the helmets of the miners cast an eerie blow over their faces and shone from their helmets, a fathering of spirits, half visualized by their helmet lights. Their skin shone in the quavering kerosene light. When they moved their heads, the ghostly aspect of the crowd became apparent. Down further into the hold, the light at the head frame was long gone. Now they moved downward though space and time for almost a half hour, it seemed, to Garvey. The lift came to an abrupt half with a bump and a lurch. Opposite Garvey, the men exited the platform by the safety gate. The superintendant carried two lanters that he placed at opposite sides of the chamber, a room of about thirty feet by twenty feet. Here and there a faint sparkle of silver-laden turquoise caught the lantern light.

The first speech came from the supervisor. He was in charge of this shift crew and was responsible for their safety in the mine. He held one of the lanterns up to inspect the clings. There was no night shift. Only day workers mined silver in the empire mine. It had been foreseen by the company officials that the rock crushers could handle only the output of the day shifts, of which there were to, each of which, work six hours.

Mr. Ronals Geyser, the super ordered two of the miners to lay out the beams for placement against the roof of the chamber. The other miners began to hack, hammer, and chip a way the rock, the sounds of the metal of their tools emitting a slight echo down in the hold. Garvey was here to gather a story for Mr. Edison of the *Eagle*. He wanted to be as thorough as he could be. People up there in the village should have a clear picture of what hard rock mining was like—the dangers, the rewards, the fears and risks, and the camaraderie. "You're the reporter for the *Eagle*," the upper announced, watching what the miners were doing, always alert to all activity down in the pit, the hole.

"Yes, sir. Name's Garvey."

"Well, Garv, what you see is the day's first shift. We work six hours then go topside for a smoke at half-time. No smoking in the mine. Eighteen, nineteen including myself. We go for the turquoise. It contains the silver, sometimes visible, often now. How do we raise the ore to the surface? That elevator you come down on with gun with six ore carts. It goes up, empties into a tram that rolls the stuff on to the crushers, then returns the empties for refills. That process goes on all day long, one shift to the next. We ain't in no hurry, you understand. But we got to make a day's wages and then some. Owners cut us a break, six hours. Some mines work eight, ten, twelve. Not us. We deliver what the crushers can handle." Garvey was scrawling down some notes in his pad, the waning light making his writing almost invisible.

"How many times a day do your men extract, Mr. Geyser."

"Fifty tons ain't unusual. The mountain is rich in silver. We do our bests, but we don't break our necks getting the stuff out of the ground."

Then in the background the metallic clash of picks and short-handled shovels filled the silence.

In the shifting and flickering light, the visages of the miners were evanescent, pale yellow. The light was deceptive in that movement was hard to discern unless one, unaccustomed to the slackening light from the scope lanterns and the lights on the mines helmets, came and went as the men moved about in the shadows and semidarkness.

"Do your dig ahead where those four are working to carve a tunnel out the mountain?"

"We followed the ore. Taink like coal with a seam of ancient plant life. Silver ore is scattered. We follow the turquoise and the silver. Sometimes the metal sparkles in the light. Often or not it's hidden in the rocks we dig out. Silver is a uncertainly metal. You can put that down. We can dig for a day in here one day and produce fifteen, thousand dollars worth of silver and the next day ten dollars. We try to outsmart the mountain."

Garvey put that down. "God knows."

"What's that."

"God knows where the silever is."

"We don't ask him none. We jes do our day's work"

"And thank God every miner is safe."

"That's right, Mr. Reporter . . . Garvey." The super turned to tend to the laying of shoring at the roof of the chamber, midway, to prevent a cave-in.

"Stand by here, Mr. Reporter." Garvey looked about him and saw men leaning on the tourney ahead. "Warning, Mr. Reporter. When you hear the cry 'fire in the hole,' hit the dirt. The miner is about to light the fuse to blow down some rocks. He might injure you, the power of the blast in this confined space."

Sure enough, "fire in the hole" came. The miners dropped their shovels and picks and pikes and hit the dirt in the tunnel just as the explosion went.

"Tiyu are really a hazard down here, Mr. *Eagle*. You don't know what's going on.

"I have my report. I did not get an interview, but the miners tell their own story."

"Good. When the cars are full, you can ride with them to the surface and finish the description of the mining for silver."

"Thanks for your help, Mr. Super."

"I'm the boss. The super is in the helmet room up above."

Garvey waited around for another hour, observing the weird movement of lights through the dust from the explosion and assuming much that would make a good story for the *Eagle*.

The cars filled. Darly took a spot behind the last car, the brass rang, and the elevator began its ascent to the surface. He glanced across the chunks of rock at the super, busy in his chamber, and then the surface. Daryl stepped off the ride and out into the clean chill air of the mountainside.

He saw the towns tin roofs emit an eerie glow in the sunlight, and then he sat it, a fire, a fire in a hay wagon down along mainstream. He skilled, scuffed up the dust as he ran, jogged down the mountain trail to the rim road, Ada Street, then across the thousand-yard Miner Street, called Bastard Road in the beginning. He ran by the wagon and observed the farmer clinging frantically to the reins to hold his horse, terrified by the fire, from bucking and running down Miner Street.

Daryl removed his knife from its sheath and clashed the harness, liberating the terrorized horse that bucked, reared, whinnied.

"Your horse, not a thousand yard distant, your horse would have set the entire town on fire."

"My harness, my harness" was all the farmer could cry.

Daryl jerked the pipe from the farmer's lips and promised, "I'll purchase a set of harness at the Bar Circle Stables T, you know, where the Royalty hole is. That's where I'm staying, drop by tomorrow. Ask the clerk. I'll have a set of harness waiting there for you, your name, sir."

"George."

"Well, see the clerk for your harness at the Royalty Hotel, tomorrow. Okay."

The farmer remained silent. Two boys and a human had begun to shovel direct into the wagon to dampen the flames and to reduce them to embers. The wagon could have been a total loss otherwise. The floorboards were replaceable.

That night he found that editor Edison had placed a small check, representing upfront money for hiring, his boss. He decided he ought the next day to pay a visit to the bank.

At midmorning he dropped into Gullivers Bank in the town, the only bank. He stepped into a situation that was terrorizing to the workers there, one of whom had her hands raised. The bank was undergoing a robbery. It did not take him long to appraise the situation. He first spotted a burlap bag standing on a counter. Youth of about seventeen was busy pouring coins from a teller's drawer into the sack. Daryl calmly went over, the slit the sack from neck to bottom with his razor bowie knife. Silver coins rolled onto the bank floor in all directions. The youth, slender blonde, shaggy hair, a masks over his eyes, cursed him for his intrusion. Daryl was down on his knees scooping the coins and putting them in the slit bag. The robber was not intimidated. He had a gun pushed under his belt.

"What in hell. This is not of your business, sir."

"Robbery?"

"What in hell does lit look like."

Down on his knees, with the robber doing the same, Daryl said to him, "Run, kid. Run for your life. You don't want to spend ten years out on Alcatraz island for this . . . bank robbery. Look at these easily coined, dollars . . . dollars. Your life is not worth it. Get up. Dust your hands. Run like hell before the sheriff comes and take you captive. Run. It isn't worth it. Ten years of your life for one dollars in coins. Bad bargain. Get up and run. I'll cover for you. Ten years on the island and you'll get out a hardened criminal. Run, kid. Run. run." The youth stood, dusted his hands, and did exactly that, running out the door. The manager came over to Daryl.

"That was smart. What you said to the punk."

"I told him to run. Ten years on the island aren't worth the few coins he'd steal."

"Good."

The manager and two more employees began to gather up the spilled coins.

"The problems with this town, Mister, is that we don't have a sheriff."

"Well, I'm a reporter for the *Eagle*. Maybe we can help."

As soon as Duval stepped through the door of Calico's only luxury four-room hotel, the International Hotel, the clerk shouted, "A farmer came and picked up your harness, Mr. Duval."

Oh, good, good. He sniffed the air. Perfume . . . flowers. He looked about the lobby. The clerk pointed to a small vase in one corner.

"Contribution of my new maid. Cynthia. A gift for flowers . . . from the surroundings. Sorta add to the lobby's looks, don't you think."

"Not many women here in town, if any. She'll be a first."

"You mind your manners, Mr. Duval."

The hotel guest regarded the clerk with a shrewd eye.

"I am a reporter, sir, not a philanderer." The word sailed over the clerk's head.

"She made your bed, sir."

"Good. I like the feminine touch. Did that farmer say anything when he picked up the harness?"

"No, sir."

"He set his hay wagon afire with smoking. His horse was terrorized . . . all he could do to hold her in check. I had to cut therein or else the rat-burning wagon would have set the whole town afire."

"You'd be surprised . . . then there's the woods three miles away. We haven't enough firemen to fight a forest fire."

"No, sir."

"I'm going up to my room."

The clerk handed Duval the key to his room.

"Oh, I almost forgot." He reached up with his chef's tongs and snatched a note from Duval's box.

Duval took the note and read it. It was an invitation by his editor Dixon and his wife to come to a welcoming dinner at their house east of Slamshell Hill. Duval stuffed the invitation into a shirt pocket and skipped up the steps to his room. He was in no mood for chatter. He left the short statured clerk watching him haunt the stairs and shook his head.

"All sorts of folks line frontier town," he murmured.

He had done enough writing for the day.

He had interviewed the five mentors of a band that had congregated to play in the What's Wrong gaming hall. A week earlier, the carpenters had nailed on the last shingle and tested the latches of the hall, regarding their polished plank floor with admiration. There were no women in Calico, but it would not be long before they arrived. There were two that Duval knew of—a washerwoman one of the minders had imported and Dixon's wife. As he sat on his bed, he recalled the session of the interview. The drummer was a stout man in a fleece-lined jerkin. His face was large, eyes pinched, a shag of white hair over one eye, and the manner of a dancing master. The band had played one piece for the reporter from the *Eagle*. A guitarist sat with a stoop and watched his strumming and pickling like a doctor in surgery. The violinist was tall, slender like a fence, paling, fierce eyes and lingers like pastry sticks in action as he played a waltz. The clarinist looked uncomfortable in his rather formal garb, as if he should be playing for a luxury band in a pricey hotel in San Francisco. They all were, in fact, importees from the city by the bay. Then there was the band master, a swarthy fella with a slickened moustache who has the aspect f a gamekeeper, watching the caged animal, as impatient and distrusting as he squinted at his band members. The music was mellow and well performed, Duval remembered. He poured a glass of water for himself from the pitched on the dresser. Now that the hotel had a maid, he could expect fresh water from the outside well every night when he returned home. He still had to find a place to bathe . . . on the lower creek. When the women came to town, as they would, slowly and reluctantly, a bathhouse would appear on the landscape.

Duval removed the invitation from his shirt pocket. The time set for the dinner was the following evening at Mr. and Mrs. Dixlon's new house on the other side of Slamshell Hill, round top that broke or impeded the stern winds from off the crags of the Sierras to the west. The winds from the elevations were at times so fierce that the carpenters had had to lay the shingles in a a certain direction on the rooftops so that the wind did not lift them and send them flying like leaves in the wind. Duval had let this thought, "Let him who doubts the agency of God be counselled." Duval was not a particularly religious man He simply wanted to care, the simplest way of putting his attitude toward other men.

The next night arrived soon enough. Duval has spent the day on an assignment once again down into the Empire Mine. He intended to interview the pit boss while the men picked and shoveled silver ore. He had often thought about the dangers of mining since he arrived in Calico. He intended to query Jack Smith about the dangers of deep-hole mining, causes of explosions, and such matters as would interest the readers of the *Eagle*.

At his hotel, Duval greeted the clerk with a nod and shuffled up to his room to attempt some sort of hygiene and cleaning for his visit to his boss's house. They would have to understand the rigors and conditions of a visit to the Empire Mine.

"For what. I'm here to investigate for a news story."

"Well, now that's a shame," said the constable. "We're here to make an arrest."

"Of me . . . for what?"

"For murder."

Duval caught his breath.

"Am I under arrest?"

"You're right on the mark there."

Sherriff pulled a frayed piece of newspaper from one pocket and showed it to Duval. "This here's yer night of killing, Mr. Sexton."

"You keep calling me Sexton. That isn't my name. I'm here in Calico to do good to others for my keep for the local newspaper. My secret name is John. I have baptised the lord. We all have our secret wishes. I call them visions. You, Sheriff, want to be a king, absolute in your declarations and you . . . Mr. Constable wish to be the advisor to someone of power, the mayor when we get one in this town. A realist, I am in the employ of Mr. Dixon here and his newspaper, the *Eagle*."

He thought for a minute he was some kind of sky bird. "Don't be funnin' with me, gents. You're holding me for murder. You got another thinking coming, gents." The constable pulled Duval to the back of the meeting hall as the three of them passed the dancing figures to an undisclosed area.

"This here's our jail, Mr. Sexton," said the constable "We're putting you in here for the night, do your nature stuff in there. There's a pot, and we'll come fer you in the mornin'."

"I'm arrested."

"That's what it's called, Mister," said the sheriff.

"You jes think about an alibi fer your murder of Gent Hiram Teston, big man in the city, 'cause we haven't got to yet but you got a lesson to learn."

"I didn't kill any man."

"Save yer of breath for the jury, Mr. Sexton. Here's yer supper," the constable said. He handed Duval a bottle of beer and slammed the door to the makeshift jail. There was no cot, no blanket. Duval slept on the floor, curled up, with his jacket pulled over his head. He was not accustomed to such harsh treatment. He was determined to make the best of his situation.

Morning came quickly enough. A small window to the storage room let in a pale dawn light. He waited for his jailers. He waited two long hours. They swung open the door without comment, and each man taking Duval by an arm, they rushed him out of the meeting hall fo the road outside. There, standing at the boardwalk, was a hearse, a black hearse drawn by a black horse and a man in rags up on the seat at the reins.

"Git in," said the constable.

Duval did as ordered and sat down on the lid of a coffin. The hearse jerked forward and began to roll. It rocked and rumbled until it drew up in front of the office of the *Eagle*.

There was a stirring about outside. The hearse door opened, and the sheriff ordered, "Get out, Sexton. Yer reporting fer work, you lying bastard."

"Stick around," the constable yelled to the driver of the hearse.

"This here's the office of the newspaper," said the sheriff. "Don't look like no newspaper office to me."

The three men stomped up onto the boardwalk, and the constable entered the front door to the *Eagle*. Dixon, the editor, sprang to his feet.

"What . . . this?" he cried.

"We got a friend, he says he works for you."

"Duval!" cried the editor.

"This yer man's name is Sexton, Ga Sexton."

"That's not his name."

"Changed his name, I suspect," said the sheriff. "Sexton is his real name."

"May I defend myself. Sorry to bring this trouble on you, Mr. Dixton. These here fellas, sheriffs from San Francisco, they accused me of murder."

"Murder . . . my reporter has murdered a man."

"You say it right," said the sheriff. "In San Francisco, at the Claremond Hotel. Stabbed the man to death."

"I don't believe it."

"'Course not. He looks respectable."

"I have never killed a man or a woman. I am innocent. Save that for the jury," said the Sheriff.

"Says his name is not Sexton," said the constable.

"Sexton is his right name," said the sheriff. "He can't hide from the law with a fake name. I've seen this before."

"He is an honest man, gentlemen. And I'm sure that he has never committed murder."

"There, you see."

"Careful, Mr. Editor," said the constable. "You don't want to be no accomplice in a murder by defending this here murderer."

"You keep accusing me of murder, without any evidence. And don't please bring out that newspaper clipping. That isn't going to persuade a jury of my guilt."

"No, we got the name of witnesses who were there that night."

"Well, come on in, let's not hold court here in my newspaper office. Sit down gents. I can assure you that Mr. Duval is an innocent man. I know men, I see their motives, I know their natures and the motives for their actions.

"Then who is he?" the constable asked.

"He is a decent, law-abiding citizen of Calico, Constable . . . and who gave you the authority to be a constable in the first place?"

The constable remained silent.

"You have a right to remain silent," said the sheriff.

"I'm glad you said that," the editor replied, "because . . . because it is a crime to falsely accuse a man of a high crime. You both can be prosecuted for making false charges against an innocent man. You know that, Sheriff, Constable. We know the law. We got our man.

"Until you can prove some that he is a murderer, even if you suspect him, and you then drag him off to jail without sufficient evidence, I shall lodge a lawsuit against the two of you. Hear me?"

"We heard," the sheriff replied.

"To falsely accuse a man of a vicious crime and then to arrest him on a mere suspicion, without tangible proof, at least of one witness, is a criminal act. I'm not your fool, gentlemen, and so I am ordering that you release this man immediately so that he can return to his work as a reporter for my paper."

The sheriff and the constable looked at each other.

"You got the wrong man. My employee here, and my friend, is not your Mr. Sexton. His name is Duval. Now I got work to do, so if you'll leave my office, I'd be much obliged."

The sheriff motioned with his head, and the two interrogators exited the newspaper office of the *Eagle*.

"I don't know."

"Say no more, Duval. They got the wrong man, by name, by circumstances. You weren't in the city that night. You were down here. The sheriff did not say the date of the alleged murder . . . or the date on that city paper, did he?"

"No, sir."

"Good, then consider that I got you out of a binding situation. Those two can be charged with false arrest, breach of the peace, slander in public, and acting without a warrant for your arrest."

"That's right, Mr. Dixon."

"Now, did you get a story from your night at the meeting hall."

"The dancers?"

"Yes."

"No women to dance with just men, but the band didn't move the men dancers out on that floor working up a sweat without a commotion for women."

"Well, make short squib of two paragraphs out of the details, Duval."

"Thank you, sir."

Duval sat down at a small table, and snatching pencil and a sheet of rats paper from the editor's desk, he began to write out his report. The composition required only a few minutes. He stood. Dixon stood. He extended his hand to his editor.

"Sorry, sir, to cause you so much trouble."

"Think nothing f it, Duval. We all make mistakes. I remember what you told us at our house." He accepted that as a declaration of innocence, a bad situation.

"The man was drunk and reckless. You have no choice other than to let him pummel and kick you down those stairs like a mangy dog. You did not intend to fatally . . . was it fatal? You do not even have proof that the man was dead."

"That's right, sir."

"Don't let your conscience lead you astray . . . to make a confession to an act that was not murder."

"That's my opinion too, sir. You saw how eager that sheriff and the constable were."

"Popular opinion leads some men into dangerous acts and undeserved charges . . . you get the cut of my saw in the matter."

"I understand, sir."

"Did I leave my hat here." He looked around him.

|You weren't wearing it when you came in . . . the black cowboys hat."

"That's the one."

"Somewhere else." The editor turned to his desk. "Now I got the paper to put out. You find a feller who has the gift of language, send him to me. I could use another reporter. He won't get right. And here, Duval, here's the pay for your story . . . and your efforts on behalf of justice and honesty. We need both in our business."

"I appreciate that, sir."

Duval left the editorial office of the *Eagle* and walked back to his hotel without incident.

When he returned to the lobby of the International Hotel, Jere, the clerk, handed him a surprise in the form of a letter. He paid the clerk for the next week's rent and mounted the stairs to his back room. He was angry and sat trembling.

*W*hen he arrived at the mortician's house, driving the stagecoach, owned by Butterfield Inc., he was surprised to find not just Harry Smith, the mortician awaiting him, for apparently the mortician had heard of the gunfire and expected this sort of outcome. Also, however, the figure of the county sherriff came out to the coach alongside the mortician.

"Well, well, if it isn't our singing deputies and gunshot wizards. Duval, Frank Duval, I got some news you might be interested in hearing."

"Nothing you can say will interest me, sir."

"Oh, come now. I'm not all bad news. The man you stabbed . . ."

"Sir, that is a supposition."

"A witness is ready to talk. The man you stabbed, or let us say, poked a little sharp fun at, has died, just last night."

"Of what cause?"

"Well, now I don't want to ruin your day, but it's my opinion . . . just a opinion, mind you . . . that he died of the same knifing that sent him to the hospital in the first place. But then that's just my opinion. I ain't the court."

"Yeah, and you've been pretending to be the judge and prosecuter all along, Sheriff."

"I always keep my doubts to m' self, Duval. I just thought I'd give you the news from the hospital."

"Thank you, Sheriff, however, we eliminated a party taking your side in the cause of robbery, stagecoach robbery. Their guns are inside."

The sheriff went to the side of the coach and flung open the door. "Heavily armed, I'd say." He reached to the pile of weapons inside the stagecoach. "What do you plan to do with all that gang's guns, Duval?"

"I think I'll give them out to newcomers here in Calico since you seem to lack support, eh?"

"I can get support when I need it."

"You don't always have time, Sheriff. Let's be realistic."

"Don't be too clever for yourself, Duval. I know where you're coming from. I can handle thugs here in Calico."

Duval was stunned into silence. After all, he was not the responsible mayor of the silver-mining town. The sheriff's territory was the county . . . or was it?

"Begging your permission, Sheriff Claxton, but but I'm going to deliver these guns . . . just as soon as I get the bodies inside on its way to the morgue."

Duval dismounted from the stage and placed the body of the dead driver on a rolling gurney the mortician had wheeled out to the stage. Duval and the mortician removed the body of the slain driver and watched it disappear into the morgue. "Now, if you will pardon my haste, Sheriff, I want to deliver this . . . this Butterfield customer and a gang member killed in the street fight. To the waiting room inside the morgue. No? Maybe you can move these stiffs before they begin to smell."

In a matter of minutes, the remaining bodies were trundled into the morgue. Duval climbed up onto the seat again and took the reins.

"Thanks for the help, Clovis," he said to his deputy who all the while had helped with the unloading.

"I'll be around, Sheriff. I'm not going anywhere." He waved at the sheriff and clucking to the team drove the Butterfield stagecoach to another part of town with his captured load of firearms. He left the sheriff staring after him in puzzled wonderment. The Butterfields did not show any of the usual signs of personal guilt for a stagecoach robbery, except that he examined the bullet holes on the coach body with intense curiosity and an expression of dismay and wonder.

Duval mounted up onto the driver's seat where a deputy sat, and together, they pitched to the ground the unusually heavy strongbox. Manner asked why the stage was so irregular. He did not need to point out the bullet holes or they were already evidence taken into account of the fury of the gunfight. The stagecoach had the appearance of a victim of spotted Rocky Mountain fever. The station manager looked inside and saw the bloody interior and was aghast. He unhitched he team and led them to a ramshackle ban. This station was not prepared to change the team for fresh horses. Duval and his deputy dragged the strongbox to the ground and carried it to the interior of the station. His work was done as the mayorasked. He told the deputy that he would meet him and the others at the boarding house and see that they were paid for their "necessary services." He would need their help in the distribution of the gang weapons to the civilians of Calico. He then went back to his hotel room to write a story about the stagecoach attempted robbery in town. As he lay back in his chair that night, he thought about the prostitute who had managed to become allied with the gang.

That cold clear night, he thought that he heard the puffs of a steam-powered saw, and he whine of the circular saw through the dry, cutting planks. That was the real night's music for the town. The small muscular man with the long face who owned the property above the mill had invested well in the row of cottages in which customers could analyze the numbers of planks cut from one log amid the night's noise. Five cottages were to be built, two stood, and one was occupied only the lady at the Silver Inn. The cold and only night of Calico closed in, and Duval fell asleep. It had been a hard and challenging day . . . as mayor and as reporter.

A DEPT HARDWARD REPORTS A drop in sales of cow bells and horse collars due to the recession in farm futures.

Mabel Comstock is running short of chicken of others for her lovely brocade pillow. She pays a dollar a pount, soaks them in alcohol—not Jack Daniels, washes them in hot sudsy water and sun dries them before she stuffs them into her heirloom pillows.

Early sleepers have complained about crowing roosters. The Invisible Rooster Silencers has come out with a rooster silencer that fits like a collar around the foul's neck and silences his cock-a-doodle-doo.

Has your horse thrown a shoe lately? Jack Farril has set up a circulating forge on the back of his wagon. Let him come to your farm and fit Betsy with a new set of road shoes. His warrantee: If your horse throws one of its shoes, he'll replace it free of charge.

Keep well with Doctor Shakes castor oil. "One spoonful does it" is his motto.

Sam Bowlson almost ran over a jumping kangaroo rat other day. Now it's a matter of training the little rascal to boum and fetch the morning paper.

The *Eagle* paper is happy to announce that it is having another window cut in the editorial room for better light and sharper vision. The paper always takes no hints from the mountain spirits.

Let a fine stallion breed your mare for one hundred dollars. The foal can be a winner at the racetrack at Las Vegas and more that can return your investment.

Shave off that long beard before it gets caught in the machine . . . at Salvo's Barbershop on Hyde Street, Calico.

Need new boots. Try 'em on at Knee Boot Shop on Hyde. Also available, revolver hoosters, boot jacks, sadle repairs and resoling those dance stompers. HJiyall Jackson.

Spindlely Smith, the blacksmith, is ready to forge your every need with his hot hammer and roaring forget at Twin Corners, Calico.

$\mathcal{N}$o sooner had Dr. Hart, with the reporter's help, delivered the injured minor into the cottage hospital, uniquely furnished in an operating table, medicine cabinets, a kerosene power beam, and other medical accessories, including a glassed in sunporch, the mine superintendant, having removed the identification tag from the crushed body of the suffering miner than he closed the gate to the platform and dropped into the hole where he spied the miners' lights at the end of the tunnel. He rushed past the half-filled ore carts and approached the pit boss Jack Quick.

"Cave-in, Mr. Hodges.

"Yes, I can see. My god, the spacing . . . don't you know eight feet between stanchions is not enough, Mr. Quick? Four feet. There's half a million tons of mountains up above, just waiting to fall into this tunnel. Four feet. Take those beams there and reinforce the tunnel bracing . . . now.

The miners, who were sitting about, sprang into action and began the job of adding stanchions to the present beams to shore the tunnel roof. The superintendent Hodges walked to the debris on the tunnel floor and scooped up a handful of sand. "See here, Mr. Quick, this sand . . . it's damp."

The super dug his hand into a cascade of sand at the fallout, fingered it, observed its dampness under his miner's lamp.

"There's water not far away, a trickle, maybe a stream and God help us an underground river. We start a tunnel in a different direction."

"Yes, sir," said the pit boss.

"At a right angle to this, back fifty yards and headed south, away from this tunnel We can only speculate the source of the dampness, the water, its volume and its direction. But we'll have to take the chance. I'm going to have a talk with the mine owner tonight. Have the men finished the shoring of the present tunnel into the next shift. When that's done, they can go home . . . wait for my call. Messy business and anything but efficient, but I'm not going to have these men drown like rats in a sewer. We've got to outsmart the nature of the business. I've got a good topographer who can trace every water source at the base of the mountain, if that exists."

"Yes, sir," said pit boss Quick

"Pass the word along. Tomorrow morning, I don't want to see any man down here until I solve the problem of where in hell is that water coming from. Okay."

"Yes, sir," said the pit boss. He turned to the men. "All of you use the timbers available," the super ordered. "Cut the distance betweens stations in half, four feet between support beams." "Okay." There came a mumble of men's voices as they worked at the task. The timbers were precut; here and there rocks were being used to wedge beneath the posts to make them tight against the beams. And so the work went on into the next shift that finished the task after midnight, the miners leaving their hand tools behind, doing their shirts, and loading onto the platform, temporarily leaving the deep, dark hole in the mountain lifeless and lightless for another thirty-six hours.

Duval returned to his hotel room after he had helped removed the crushed miner from the doctor's ambulance cart.

"His chances of survival?"

"Loss of blood was the worst part. The trauma. I could use some help. I'll have to put his legs in a cast by myself. I can do it, but . . . well, I'll put him under a sedative anesthesia. I can manage."

So Duval stayed throughout the night, helping the doctor in routine matters and leaving the cottage in the early morning, the patients legs set and in casts. It had been a difficult night, since the elimination of paint totally was not possible. The groans of the injured miner struck to the core of both men as they worked over the near-lifeless victim of the cave-in. The doctor was spooning some slight nourishing into the patient's lips when Duval wished the doctor the help of God in his new task.

"If I meet anything who could help, I'll pass the word along, Dr. Hart."

"Thank you, Mr. Duval."

"Godspeed, sir." Duval with that parting left for his hostel room to write his story.

He was not a drinker, but he pulled a bottle of wine from the cupboard and took three or four hefty swallows. He pulled up a chair to the table, fished a pencil from his jacket pocket and a tablet from his gear, which he had not full unpacked at this point.

He first described the mine as the *Eagle* readers requested of the editor, and then he went into a description of what had occurred, the collapse of the shoring in the mine roof, inadequate for the situation. He described the miners—their sweaty, bearded appearances, their shirtless torsos even though the year-round temperature was 58 cool degrees. He then went into detail about the sudden fallout of the rock and the entrapment of one miner named Tim. That was all he knew about the man. His legs, both legs, had been trapped by the rock fall; and it took two men with prybars to free him. The trapped victim was futurnate that the rock fall had not covered him. The poor fellow now lay in a bed at the cottage hospital of Dr. David Hart.

Duval finished his story about midnight. He threw himself across the bed and was soon fast asleep in an exhausted slumber.

When he awoke at daybreak, Duval washed his face in the basis provided by the hotel. He had a bowl of hot porridge at the Sasparilla bar and cafe over in Fiske street. Thus he did, walking slowly, enjoying the fresh morning air that always revealed the wintry weather atop the crags of the Sierras that rose above the town. Only the sight of wafting fog air from the frozen summit told him that the weather would remain warm and calm, even though the winter was approaching. It would arrive earlier than it arrived at lower elevation.

He entered the Lackadaisy Cafe and ordered hot cereal, this time oatmeal with fresh milk and a cup of steaming coffee. He ate in silence. That waiter was a male, as he had expected. There still were no signs of women in the town, a fact that surprised him, since carpenters had begun to build a one-room schoolhouse not far away from Fiske street. There was the anticipation of families moving to Calico . . . but when was anybody's guess.

On the morning after the accident and before his reporter had turned in his story, Dixon and his wife Edna had arisen and were enjoying their breakfast in their small cottage on the outskirts of Calico. Duval is a good reporter. Readers will get a picture of what happens down in a mine.

That should be exciting.

"What do you think of him, Edna? He's been here once. You have just met him."

"Good reporter, young, energetic. Keep him, I may say so. He asks no special privileges, that's what I seemed to detect."

"How's that?"

"He's aggressive by nature."

"Good. That's a quality of a good reporter. We've got to keep people interested in the *Eagle*. When it gets to sound like a political report from Sacramento, we'll lose readers. Nothing wrong with politics, is there, dear?"

"No, not usually, until they grow weary with details. A good political fight is always newsworthy. Duval always seems to be on a scene where he can help."

"Better than being a collaborator for or a saboteur or a-a . . . malcontent of some sort."

"Maybe we can ask the seer."

"Seer? Have you forgotten. I've already asked a dozen people to the welcoming party."

"I didn't know Calico needs a seer," Dixon replied.

"Oh, yes. Every growing town needs a professional seer. Tabor Mohammud has had his presence known. I've personally invited him next friday to come here, meet my guests, and perhaps tell one or two fortunes. Invite Duval. Let's see what Mr. Muhammud has to say about your star reporter."

"He's no star, Edna. He's just, well, he's ways available."

"Exactly. Perhaps, just maybe he can tell us a little more about Duval, a reporter for the *Eagle*."

"Well, I won't enter his remarks into the paper or into Mr. Duval's work record. I tell you, privately. I have heard that he killed a man. I'd rather you now. I'm sorry I told you. I have no proof."

"He has no family."

"Girlfriend . . . his fiance . . . in San Francisco."

"Is he a suspect, or do they know for certain?"

"I don't know, Edna. Right now . . . just a rumor. I don't know where I heard it."

Duval dismissed the image of his charge for the man's wounds bearing upon a night he remembered well. As a reporter in a small Sierra town, he wanted to make good in his profession and marry his sweetheart. The best solution, he concluded, as he read her letter cautioning silence, was to gather together a cadre of some four to six men who could follow instructions. They would visit the various businesses in Calico and,for a very small fee, caution them against bandits, robbers in the town, malcontents, and roaming rogues who sought to kill and to plunder. Calico was a special target for such agents of violence. He put Anna's letter alway and sat down to reply to her words of caution

"Dear Vivian. No matter my words of intent in this letter, remember that I love you and I always shall. We belong together . . . but not right now. You would not be safe in Calico. There is too much violence, intentional, and brought about carelessness for you to live a happy and safe life here with me. We are close and shall always remain so. Love forever, Duval."

He sealed the letter and took it downstairs where he handed to Jere. He would put his plan into operation in the morning. He had no assignment from the paper's editor, Mr. Dixon.

An entrepreneur had constructed a rickety, hastily built boarding house for itinerant miner in the town. It was there he went the following day to begin to muster his small clique of enforcers. He spent little time there, acquired a list of the seven tenants, made himself known to the management as a newspaperman and left the building. He would need some fine clothes, those befitting a mayor godfather. He had decided to combine the office with the action in the hyphenated signature. Duval, mayor. He stopped by the press office where the *Eagle* was printed and arranged for a stamp and a business card, a calling card it is called, to indicate his new profession as a self-chosen mayor of Calico. At the outfitters, where other items such as leather vests, boots, and hunters caps and jackets were sold, he got outfitted with a fine business suit for those occasions when he felt that either he should take a public appearance or call upon one of his constituents. All of this self-magnification was gaining acceptance in his own mind and the details of which he was adding by the hour and the day, for he was in a second day of his, he chuckled at the thought, his term of office.

Vivian would be proud of him in his new suit, and she could come to accept his new station as the mayor, protem, self-appointed, de facto of the small silver mining town of Calico, California. He strode from the haberdasher's shop, the outfitters, down toward the office of the *Eagle*. When he opened the door and stepped inside, the editor gasped, his jaw fell, and he scanned his reporter from his head to toe and back again.

"Well, what have we to thank for this transformation, Mr. Duval?"

"My ambition to be, at least, to look like I have a place in a wild western town . . . and you must admit, sir, Calico is a wild western town."

"Sometimes more than others," said Dixon.

"I am the acting mayor . . ."

"Appointed by . . . you know we have no city council."

"Appointed by God."

"Oh, come now, Duval. You can't be serious."

"I am serious, sir."

"What exactly do you hope to accomplish by this charade."

"Sir, this is not a charade. I have seen so much near violence caused by carelessness and by personal bad luck that I wish to try to correct what I have witnessed. You know where I have saved the life of a mother and her babe, the incept the entire town of Calico from catching fire, preserve the life of a boy from a life of criminal penal hardship by intruding in his robbery . . . and others."

"I know from that night at my house that the deputee had his eye on you. I think you mentioned why."

"That was a comedy of errors, sir. My fiance will witness for me."

"Perhaps so, Duval. But . . . you look very official and important, more than a reporter should."

"Sir?"

"Mayor. I shall put quote marks around that. Of course, a man has a right to pretend to be anything he wants. I can pretend I am a magician, like that seer. I can foretell the future of Calico as well as he . . . trouble, yes."

"That exactly why I have chosen to . . . to adopt a new visage."

The editor grimaced with Duval's choice of words . . . a visage.

"All right, you look more in style, perhaps for some assignments in that . . . fine suit."

Duval pretended to make manly gesture of posing.

"It fits, it costs little."

"I shall have assignments . . . perhaps more in the mines, in the dance shall, in the shops of the harness maker, the ferrier, and wheelwright. You shall look great. You will represent the *Eagle* . . . as its owner, heh?"

"So I shall go about the business of gathering news in Calico, sometimes in my mayor's garb."

"Mayor . . . good lord, what next!"

"I am thinking of hiring another reporter. The town is growing by leaps and bounds, and the news will not wait."

"That's fine. I applaud your decision, sir. Meantime, do not hesitate to give me assignments. I can shuck this gentleman's suit and return to the mines, as it were."

"Glad to hear you say that, Duval. Now . . . oh, yes, I do have an assignment, tonight . . . and you can wear your fine suit, at the new casino in the Crags Hotel . . . the red brick structure just finished. There's something the people of Calico should know . . . good business. There's a casino."

"I know, sir. A man was shot there night before last. I saw him lying on the sidewalk."

"You think he was shot in the casino?"

"Quite possibly, sir. I am going to put a halt to this sort of violence."

The editor turned away with a glance of suspicion to his paperwork on his desk.

Duval returned to the boarding house, the Silver Rock Boarding House. His plan was together with his crew, as he called them, as soon as possible, they would be able to earn real dollars from their work for him. Also, he needed to spread the word about that he was the new mayor of Calico.

$\mathcal{A}$s Duval walked along the boardwalk in the direction of the rugged Sierra mountains that rose up before him, he felt a sharp, soft breezes on his face. It was a sign to the newcomers to Calico that the crags foretold the weather, that a wind from off their rugged slopes forecast either a light snowfall or a severe continuum of icy blasts from the rocks that soared 15,000 feet above the growing mining town of Calico.

This young man, new to Calico, a reporter on the street, saw a mother pushing a baby buggy close to the dirt road, while at a distance of several hundred yards a heavy-logging wagon, drawn by four horses, clopped and rumbled down the road in the same direction. Duval heard a sharp crack that struck his attention like the crack of a whip. He looked toward the road and saw one, perhaps two, of the stakes that cradled the immense load of logs snap and fall off the truck to one side. The driver slowed his rig to look back as the logs began to shift on the truck bed. The mother and her babe were almost opposite the truck and dangerously close to the shifting logs. One of the logs tended to spin while another, loosened from its bond to the load, started to roll off the open side of the truck that has almost come to a stop. The young man sprang toward the hapless woman and her carriage. Swift with agile, young vigor, he snatched the baby and its crib with one fell swoop, protecting the mother with his body as best he could, under the truck just as the log rolled off and smote the dust in the road beside the truck, crushing the baby carriage. The freed log continued continued to roll as the logging wagon came to a slow stop. Only someone who had seen the incident would swear that it actually happened. Meantime, in the flash of the seconds of emergency action, Duval, the mother, and the infant huddled in curled-up, cramped positions, expecting the worse, beneath the carriage of the wagon, the wheels of which had responded to the weak braking and the powerful back-thrust of the horses in their shafts. As Duval watched the wheels approach, he scooted himself and his burden so as to just miss the wheels of he wagon before they came to a stop. He moved the mother out from the opposite side, looking to see that the stakes on that side were still in their positions and had not splintered. He handed the babe to its mother. She managed a stiff smile and a muttered "thank you, sir." She appeared to be unhurt. She cuddled the babe carefully. She clasped the babe to her breast and went on her way. Duval stepped to the opposite side of the wagon and said to the driver.

"That was a narrow escape, driver. Your load was badly secured in the first place, sir. No chains. Ropes don't do it. The damn logs shifted, broke the ropes, and snapped the struts."

"I know. They put heaviest log atop the pile."

"There are stupid men in this world. Let me make a suggestion. Throw chains over the load and lock the links. Replace those damned wooden side stakes with iron pipes. Next time you might not be so lucky." Duval tapped his hat and continued on his way. He wrote the story of his experience the story that night for his paper, putting the emphasis on the lack of safety measures in transporting fifteen-inch diameter logs from the woods to the mill.

A woman and her infant were walking along Miner Street last Friday, taking in the fresh mountain air when a logging truck experienced a loss of control of its logs. Two of the side stakes snapped. Logs skewered and shifted on the load. One began to fall, snapping the wooden stakes that held the load on the wagon. But for the passing resident, one of the logs would surely have crushed a woman and her infant as they walked alongside the logging wagon. The driver was aware of the impending accident when he heard the stakes snap.

Such accidents should not be common. Logs should be enclosed between iron stanchions and the logs. themselves. Should be encircled by heavy chains to prevent such deadly incidents from happening in the future.

The article was short but a severe warning to readers of the *Eagle*.

When he handed his story in to Editor Dixon, the editor scratched his graying head and shook it in disbelief. He regarded his reporter with wonder and unspoken respect, except to say to Duval, "Lady luck won't always be there when you summon her, my friend."

"That's the chance I take, Mr. Dixon. I had to act. I couldn't just stand there and watch those logs roll off and crush the woman and her babe, now could I? I was close enough to act. I've seen how logs act when they start to roll and snivel around and escape out of control . . . sometimes kill the horses, men working on the logging deck. You can imagine, sir."

"Glad you were there, Duval. Readers want to know a little more about mining up at the Empire Mine. Mind taking a run up there and see what's going on. Give us a little description. Helps sell papers."

"I do that, Mr. Dixon . . . first assignment in the morning."

He greeted "Shorty", the front desk clerk's desk, took a little in hand, sniffed it, saw that Terese had on several other occasions tried to persuade him to join her in the big city, but he had failed to be convinced by the two letters she had written to say that Calico was just another small town like in the small town of the midwest and that that it was beleaguered by all sorts of gamblers and "wild people" that their existence in the town would be both dangerous and threatening to her kind and generous nature. He had failed to convince her of the realities of the scenes he saw every day, scenes that would kindle her imagination and change her outlook on life, instances of physical assault, theft, violence of every description—from fistfights in the street to dog fights and almost daily shootings—together with the hovering darkness of men without souls. He would never convince her of these realities. It was as if he actually did not want her to join him in Calico. That was the truth of their relationship, without bells or whistles. In fact he himself believed in the God-man image motto for all mankind's salvation, but what in blazes was the image of God? One had to think in reverse, that God was and exists in man's form in order for ordinary mortals to understand the analogy.

"God is watching over your conscience, my beloved Bruce," she wrote to him. "And I must also ask him to watch over mine since I am an image made in his likeness." He somehow detested those biblical rendition on life, as if scripture always stood as an indictment upon man, despite his best efforts and acts of achievements. He did not want her to come to Calico and settle in as one of its citizens. He feared not just for the harsh realities that would buffet her life's attitudes should he bring her to Calico to settle among the residents. He feared for her life because it was often factually true that in the pit of evil few survive without either becoming like the vipers that infected society in a rude, start-up mining town. Or then again, there was the danger that one might be so self-possessed by his faith. so religious as to no longer sustain relationships with neighbors and citizens. Instead, one could become like the monitors of evil empty pulpits seen almost everywhere. Was he totally lacking in sound common sense? Or had had he, Bruce Duval, become so influenced by barbarism that he was no longer capable of sane thought and compassionate relationships with townsmen.

These thoughts, now and at other times, had coursed through his conscience. Although he tried to think of himself as the best of men, he somehow seemed to gravitate toward the worst. It was not impossible that men could be reformed, but by whom, when, and in what manner? He must try to dissuade his fiancee to stay in San Francisco, a city whose Barbary Coast was never the epitome of goodness, compassion, or salvation. The Barbara Coast had made of virtue a barbarism and of barbarism a virtue. He sat down a the table in his barely furnished room and began to write a letter to her.

Dearest Terese.

You think you know me. If we were to live together, as husband and wife, you would see a different man. I pray that will happen some day. You would have to contend with the society I find here in Calico, about which is dangerous even for me. Only please, dearest, put aside thoughts of marriage until we find each other on a more common ground. Keep well. Remember what I said about the Barbary Coast. It has stamped itself permanently on 'Frisco. Peace, please do not attempt to come here to Calico. There is no place here you can stay that would be either congenial or safe. Love as always, Bruce. I am still being pursued.

He put the letter into an envelope, sealed it. That night he slept poorly, thinking of what he had written and if he had wounded her. After a restless night, he awoke, dressed, and set off for a sandwich at the Sarsaparilla Grill in lower Calico. His assignment this day was activity down in the Empire Mine.

The thought of his editor that his luck would someday run out on him troubled his mind. More importantly, it seemed to animate the appeal by his fiancee that she come to Calico where they could be married, if they could find a pastor or a priest somewhere in the town. He was not so ill acquainted with evil that he could dismiss it as an empty concept of religionists and, instead, accept the proposition that men are included to do wrong, not evil, make mistakes rather than intentional wickedness and find themselves trapped in circumstances for which only an army or the sheriff or a religion can remove them.

These thoughts were brushed away with the same chill wind gusts from the crags that had washed over his face on the morning when he rescued the woman and her babe in the street. He made it along the rocky well-tramped path that snaked back and forth up the side of the mountain to the mine shaft entrance where the gray timbers of the mine head stood out sharply against the broken granite of the brown mountainside. He walked with his head bowed and almost ran into one of the miners on the same trail. They fell into conversation between the panting exertions of the short trek up to Empire Mine.

"Finding much silver these days?" Daryl asked the miner.

"Pockets . . . lots of the blue ones . . . of value if you can find the right jewelry maker, designer of women's clothes or men's shirts. Little elegant, not much market for it."

"But the silver, do the mine owners let you keep any percentage of the silver?" Daryl asked the miner.

"Oh, no, only the super estimates what a man has discovered in a day, and if it's great, he increases his pay, if little . . . well." The miner shrugged.

"What's the worst thing that can happen when you're down there in the mine . . . oh, by the way, I'm a reporter for the *Eagle*. I expect you've read it. It's the only newspaper in town. Only . . . I ask out of curiosity."

"Curiosity has closed many a mine, mister. Oh, I suppose . . . there being methane explosion . . . bad can be a cave-in."

"A cave-in . . . ."

"Traps the miners . . . traps even one miner."

"Caused by . . . an explosion."

"No, like I say, we got no methane problem. But if we don' shore up the roof of that tunnel . . . blewee, the whole damm mountain comes roaring down inside the tunnel, and more often than not it cuts off the men from their picks and shovels . . . and their rescuers."

"And the dynamite."

"Wrong time to use dynamite, Mister Reporter. Dig, dig, and pray for the best. If the tunnel is short, the fall-in cuts off their air, if it's way down the tunnel, well . . . maybe they got a chance. I seen men try to better a cave-in and they always get crushed. Hang tight . . . drop . . . cover yer head. You can be buried . . . but you gotta go some day."

"I see. Luck."

"Fores night, sir. Timber the mine right and chances are it won't happen. Pack them beams in close. There's a whole mountain up above jes waitin to fall in on us . . . here's the shaft."

The miner rang for the elevator cart. "It's the way. We can all go down at once." Fifteen more miners stood, lunch pails in hand, waiting for the life to come up from the darkness. "We got different times, same schedule, but well, some of the guys they be drinkin the night before and cant get up in time. You understand how it is."

"Yep. I understand."

"We gotta stop at the super's shed. He'll give you a helmet and a tag number That's so's to identify yer corpse case you git killed in the mine."

"Risky business."

"You hit it, stranger. Risky. Insurance is high. Here."

They stepped off the platform. The sight Duval had seen on the prior visit greeted his eyes, the row of burning lights in helmets, the tag board with the brass tags shining in the quivering light, and the superintendent in horn-rimmed glasses who grabbed from the line of helmets a helmet for the *Eagle* reporter. The crew of inners stepped off the elevator and, finding their personal helmets, plucked his individual numbered brass tag from the tag board. The shift of miners hastily reassembled on the mine-shaft platform, ready to descent into the darkness where they would continue the work of the night shift.

"Usual rules," said the super. "We're into a part of the mountain that has sand layers . . . old ocean, I suspect. The sand makes the shoring weak. Be careful. Take care, inspect the bore sand. Remember . . . silver forms by ancient heat in the ground. Sand's fer beaches and fishermen, not fer you miners," the superintendent warned.

The superintendent closed the elevator gate; a distant bell rang for the start down. The taut cables quivered in the faint light and began their distant sling as the platform slowly got under way in its drop into the black pit. Duval was aware of rock walls of total black rising up past the floor of the elevator as it descended. After what seemed to be a perilously long time, the elevator came to a stop in the blackness of the shaft. At a distance he saw the helmet lanterns of miners at the seam in the end of the tunnel waiting to go off shift. Six ore cars stood half-filled with the debris of the miners' work.

"Here we are," said his companion. "The shift boss is standing over there . . . case you want to talk to him fer yer story . . . ." "A rotund figure of a man in short sleeves, the shift boss, emerged from the murk. He wore a yellow vest for easy identification. Duval walked over to him and introduced himself.

"I was down here once before. I'm a reporter for the *Eagle* newspaper in Calico. Folks would like to know what exactly goes on down here in a silver mine, what silver mining is like in the day of a miner."

"Well, look around you. Eight finished night's work and 're ready to go up for breakfast. You jest got off with the day shift . . . Mister . . . ."

"Duval."

"Mr. Duval. Whether hit's for silver or fer coal. Mining is mining," he spat. "Four yet to come. They'll be docked for being late. What you see is what it's about, sir. You want an interview, you come to the right man. I can tell you the same things as they all kin tell you. They're too busy to jabber." The instant bell rang again, and the departing shift started on the elevator to the superintendent's shed where they would leave their helmets and tags, then on to the surface and morning light.

The shift boss, the mine boss actually, wandered off toward his crew of fifteen day-shift men. Duval watched the miners begin their work at the seam end of the tunnel. Four of the men were involved in shoring up the roof of the tunnel with heavy twelve by twelve timbers that had been tacked along the way. The men began to shore up the roof. Incalculable tons of rock and sand pressed down above the mine tunnel, awaiting a weakening created by the miners in their excavation with picks and shovels and pry bars. That kind of mountainous pressure would identify any unprotected weakness in the substrata, such as that caused by tunneling.

Duval scribbled key words in a writing pad, by which he would write his story of the activity of miners in their day of mining for silver in the Empire Mine.

He heard a shout. He looked toward the end of the tunnel and saw nothing. Then came more shouts, the clang of metal, the rumble of stone that poured onto the tunnel floor. He heard a shout that was more like a scream. The mine boss ran toward the rock fall and the dust that momentarily obscured the miners.

"Hands on. Help me. Tommy's got caught under the fall. Oh, God." The shift boss summoned nearby miners to the site where one of them, Tommy, the clipper had been caught beneath sand and rock.

"Shovel some of that rock. Hey, you men, shovels. Tommy's caught. Grab his belt a couple a you guys, his arms at the shoulders and let's pull. Shovel some more." A pause of silence. The victim moaned. "Sure, sure, Tommy, me man. We'll get you freed in just a minute or two." The miner moaned again, giving evidence that he was seriously injured.

"That pry bar!" shouted the shift boss. "O'Malley." One of the men began to work on a large rock that lay upon the victim's legs. It was excruciating work, amid the cries of pain and the blood that now began to show through the debris.

"Keep at it, men. He's coming. We have you out of there in jus' another minute or two, Tommy, m' lad." The work continued for another several minutes, sounds of the scraping of the shovels against fallen stone filling the silence, the shifting of debris with the work, the movements of the men as they tugged at the body of their comrade.

"Hang on, Tommy. Grit your teeth a mite. It'll soon be over." At last the miners succeeded in freeing the body of their injured friend, whom they called Tommy, the clipper. He was a young man, in his thirties, small of frame yet a good worker. He had just happened to be standing in the wrong place when the weakened roof fell in upon him. Duval realized, with his inexperience, that had the man been standing a foot or more in toward the undug part of the funnel that he would have been buried and dead by this time. The miners could not continue working with one of their comrades buried; the idea was absurd and cruelly real. Now Duval stood beside the stretcher that had leaned against one wall. Upon it lay the injured man, moaning continuously out of the pain of his terrible injury. The men stood back and watched in teeth-grinding, empathetic, and painful silence.

"You six go with Tommy," said the mine boss. Duval stood beside the injured man with the six miners at the stretcher at last, after interminable minutes, loading upon and riding the elevator to the surface. What could happen next? Only the one doctor, a Dr. Hart at his village "hospital," so-called since it was only his home, only he, had the remedy for pain, the instruments, the surgical gauze, the oils and medications to prevent infection, and most important, the skill to set the leg, perhaps both crushed legs and ultimately to save the life of little Tommy the Clipper, brave miner in the Empire silver mine.

"He's in shock," said Duval. He removed his jacket and placed it over the man's torso. One of the miners removed his denim jacket and did the same, elevating the feet slightly.

"Now what?" one of the miners asked. "There's no other way. I know where the doctor's house is. I'll have to make the run. It'll take me less than an hour . . . keep him awake. Do not let him fall asleep . . . or we may just have a dead man. He's still in shock." With these calloused yet calculated instructions, Duval began his run to the doctor's house. It took him a good half an hour to make the run to the village "hospital." Dr. Hart's home was simply a cottage with a glassed-in porch and an interior equipped to care for patients in emergencies, with a surgical table, a cabinet that contained elemental medications, and a few hand tools such as a scalpel, tweezers, stitching materials, crutches, and a crude wheelchair.

Dr. Hart was at home this morning. He was working in his laboratory. Duval, breathless from his run, hammered on the cottage door. Dr. Hart knew by the urgent sound of the blows that there was need for quick action. He ran to the door. Duval explained the nature of his mission, the kind of injury a man had sustained down in the mine. He did not speculate; he was not trained to do so except to relate that the man's legs were crushed and that he was bleeding from his injury. Dr. Hart seized a great coat from a hook, thrust his arms into it, went to his cabinet, and removing a vial of morphine from a shelf, dropped it and a needle into his black bag nearby.

"Come," he said to Duval. The two of them went outside and mounted into a cart that stood hitched to a gray horse outside the cottage, Hart's primitive version of an ambulance. It was outfitted to carry two stretchers behind the cab, especially designed and welded for just such occasions as he now experienced.

The two of them mounted up into the hospital cart, which stood always ready at the front gate. The trip up the mountain was a rocking and rolling course along the ore cart tracks. Within twenty minutes, they arrived at the mine head structure. The doctor ran to the stretcher and, pausing to listen for the man's breathing, felt for his caroteid pulse and examined the injury under the blanket. He raised up and, hustling back to his cart, took his black bag to the stretcher where, opening it, he held the syringe needle needle to the morphine and withdrew ten cc's of the fluid, injecting it into the crushed miner's lower extremity in two places.

"What's the man's name?" he asked one of the miners who stood close by, watching every action of the doctor.

"Tommy, Tommy is his name, Doctor," said one of the miners.

"Well, Tommy, we've got a trip ahead of us." He saw that Tommy was alive and conscious. He would have to sustain the pain of the rocky return of the horse ambulance, along the ore-cart route. Four of the watching miners, at the doctor's instruction, lifted the injured man onto the rack at the rear of the ambulance cab. When the injured miner was secured in the cart, the doctor threw a heavy ruglike blanket over the patient before starting off down the mountain toward his cottage.

"You," said Hart, pointing to the reporter, "come with me. I'm going to need some help."

Duval dropped in beside the doctor in his horse cart, and they were off to the cottage hospital, the injured man, Tommy, moaning in excruciating pain all the way.

*N*ow that he was up and around, he thought it prudent and cordial that he pay a visit to the two families who would supply three children for the classroom at the new schoolhouse. After all, this weekend approaching was the day for the dedication of the schoolhouse as a vital and important part of the growing town of Calico. Children were like seasoning in a community, especially in a small town for they added a kind of zest, human interest, and expectation to the life of a small town. Christmas would be empty without them. And so Duval set off to the edge of the town, northward from its center, to the abode, a small frame structure recently occupied by Mr. and Missus Jack Hampton. Their children were two boys.

No sooner had Dr. Hart, with his volunteer's help, picked up the crank phone from the wall than the young volunteer, under Hart's care for epilepsy, produced the doctor's bag and set it on the operating table. One miner only, thank God, had been trapped under the rockfall. When he and Duval, with the doctor's assistant, placed the injured man on the operating table, Dr. Hart gave the man a hard, steady, and close scrutiny, pain on his face as he prepared to treat the bleeding victim of an accident that no one could help and really ever foresee. He was still alive. That was the important thing. The morphine he had a chance to be fully effective. Dr. Hart's response was courageous, animated by skill and a sense of human suffering. Over the phone he had reminded the superintendant, "Let the miners and the pit boss blanke the men before he comes to me . . . or he'll arrive a corpse. Understood?" Dr. Hart had met the victim, several miners, and Duval at the mine head with great apprehension. A crushing wound was almost inoperable and subject to gangrene. His fears were confirmed as he looked at the pathetic figure of the miner, stretched out on the bloody operating table in the cottage hospital. From the moment when he had set out for the mine head, Duval the messenger beside him, for Duval, unaware of the crank phone, had made a heroic rundown the ore-cart trail to the hospital, Dr. Hart had been aware of the possibility that others had not yet noticed, like the poor victim of his rescue, been also rapped by the cave-in.

Crushed limbs were a special kind of injury. Dr, Hart had studied the nature of such injuries in medical school. One of the chief dangers was gangreme caused by the interruption of the blood circulation. A second danger and threat to life was shock, and the third, calling up on both skill and the doctor's humanity was the professional consideration given to the man's outlook, his spiritual response, especially if the injured man wore a cross or other religious symbol about his neck. Hart realized what some are unaware of . . . that human closeness, kind voices, whispered encouragement have a healing power. The injured miner did, in fact, wear a gold cross matted in sweat and blood, for he had arrived drenched in his blood. Because there was no priest or minister nearby, Duval said a hasty prayer for the man's recovery and his strength to endure the pain of his injury. Duval thanked God, and that was the end of it. He had shared a foxhole faith possibly with a dying man. Duval was fairly certain that the miner had heard him, thus making a small contribution toward the miner's recovery. The saviors of a man's life could always contribute to, and were a part of, the resiliance of the human mind and body in any sort of bone-crushing accident of this sort.

Back at the mine, the inspection of the debris had begun long ago. "Yes, I can see. My god! The spacing . . . don't you know eight feet between stanchions is not enough, Mr. Quick? The shft boss knew a principle of mine-tunnel shoring. Four feet. There's half a million tons of mountain resting on that damned eighteen-inch beam! just waiting to fall into this tunnel. Four feet. Men, all of you, take those beams there and reinforce the tunnel bracing. Now!" The miners, who were sitting about, sprang into action and began the job of adding stanchions to the cross-over beams, to shore up and strengthen the tunnel roof. The pit boss walked to the debris on the tunnel floor and scooped up a handful of sandy rocks. "See here, gang. this rock . . . it's damp."

Other miners shoved their hands into the roof, cascade of rocks and sand at the fall-out. Mr. Quick fingered the drift in his hand while letting the dirt comb through his fingers. He observed its dampness under his miner's lamp. Several of the miners flashed their helmet lanterns on the break in the roof. The tunnel was alight with the weird, agitated shifting light beams from the helmets. Others not having participated in the rescue were sitting alongside the tunnel, watching the removal of the critically injured man.

"There's water not far away, a trickle, maybe a stream, and God help us! Maybe underground river. We start a tunnel in a different direction . . . or we can all drown like rats." He glanced at the sixteen or seventeen miners seated on the floor of the tunnel, their lamps flickering in a random drift of air down the shaft.

"Yup . . . . wet,", the pit boss confirmed. Quick studied the break in the roof where the rupture had occurred, preceded by the terrifying sound of cracking rock. Quick's studied scan was grim and fearful. "We can only speculate the source of the damp, the water, volume . . . its direction. But I've got to to take the chance. I'm gonna talk to the mine owner, tonight. Finish the shoring . . . no more mining today. When shoring is done, you can go. Wait for me to come by. Messy business and no place for water . . . in a mining tunnel! You've earned it. We can count ourselves lucky we didn't break into an underground river. Say yer prayers. You come back to work when I think it's safe to mine. We've got to outsmart nature in this business. I've got a good topographer who can trace every water source at the base of the mountain, if a water table exists. Pass the word along," the pit boss said. "Tomorrow morning, I don't want to see any of you men at the mine head until I get to the bottom of the problem . . . where in hell that water is coming from. Okay?" He watched the expressions of the idle miners, somber, intelligent, ready. "All of you . . .

finish work on those shore beams. Cut the distance between support stanchions in half . . . four feet between supports. Okay?"

There came a mumble of voices from the miners as they set to their assigned task. The travese support beams were precut. Here and there a miner pounded a rock into a crack to wedge beneath the posts to make them stable against the cross beams. The reinforcement went on into the next shift and finished the task after midnight. The miners leaved rock-brightened tools along the wall and struggling into their shirts then loaded onto the elevator platform, leaving the dark hole in the mountain lifeless and lightless for another thirty-six hours. Duval intended to return to his hotel room after he had helped the crushed miner from the doctor's to the one-horse ambulance cart.

The crushed miner's chances of survival were precarious because there was no emergency remedy for the loss of blood . . . the worst part of the traumatic accident. Dr. Hart could use some professional help. In such a primitive society as a small-town mining community, risk was a chief ingredient of existence, even though all circumstances appeared to be going normally within the town.

"I have to cast his legs by myself . . . if they're worth saving," the doctor said in a low voice to himself. "Poor fellow, God help him . . . and me!" Dr. Hart put the injured miner under a mild anesthesia, whispering in his ear to breathe deep. "I can manage. I can manage," Hart kept saying to himself.

Duval, having ridden in the ambulance down to the cottage hospital, thought he should stay for as long as Hart could use him . . . if necessary, for the night. He had no urgent business, and this was truly a sensational story for readers of the *Eagle*. Duval throughout the excitement and helping the doctor in medical-care matters planned to leave the cottage in the early morning once the patient's legs were set in casts.

The clock was slow. The windy mountain night had had been cold with the promise of snow. Duval fetched two extra blankets to cover the patient. The groans of the miner struck to the heart of the night watchers. They came to the bedside and looked down on the gravely injured body, still breathing and living. Dr. Hart shook his head in pathos and dismay. Duval read his mind and his intentions as to what. For the physician was the next thing to do for a patient who lay there, inert, groaning from time to time in pain, through the pain vaguely aware of his condition and wishing for death to come. His pulse appeared to stop, causing the doctor with his stethoscope to rise up with a start, feel for the femoral artery. He opened one eyelid, placed his ear close to the man's nose. He shook his head, looking his assistant in the eyes with a solemn stare and shot a glance at Duval that portended death. The doctor sniffed the air that hovered over the miner's crushed legs, a move that revealed bleeding through the two legs casts. The situation obviously was extremely grave, the miner being on this cold October night the near-lifeless victim of a cave-in.

The doctor's assistant had prepared and was attempting to spoon some slight nourishing broth into the patient's lips. Duval wished the doctor the help of God.

"If you need any nonprofessional help, I'm as close as the *Eagle* office. This accident is a true news story for the townspeople, sir."

"Yes, yes, Mr. Duval."

"Godspeed, Dr. Hart!" The reporter left for his hotel room to write his news story about the mine-tunnel cave-in.

Andy, the doctor's assistant, a youth with the face of an old man yet quick in stride and action, provided Hart with a chair at the patient's bedside, where he sat for one long hour, his stethoscope draped over his neck, from time to time feeling the aortic heart pulse in his patient's neck artery, then his femoral artery at the inside top of the man's leg. Hart then fell asleep again He struggled with his conscience, debating within himself whether to let the man die or to save his life by amputating his crushed legs, for it was clear that the crushed legs would not live again. The stench was evidence that they had begun to decay with gangrene. The stench of gangrene came from under the covers. The patient would surely die within hours if he, a surgeon, did not operate . . . but of what use was a man with no legs? He resolved to save as much of each leg as he possibly could, cutting halfway between the hip joint and the knee.

He awoke, saw his assistant sitting on the other side of the bed, and sent him to find a spool of suture thread and a tray of gauze, and to prepare his instruments, including the saw for cutting the patient's thigh bones. If the patient's life was worthless without his legs, why try at all to save him? For a life of agony? "Andy, can you watch a man that is having his legs cut off?"

"Hard to say, Doctor. Let me take a couple of swigs of whiskey, and I think I can to rough it."

"The same for me." The doctor bowed his head. He wanted to pray, but he had had no experience with God since his boyhood days. His conscience was involved . . . to save a man's life for its worthless existence or let him die a whole man from his injuries. Who was he to set limits on the future life of an amputee? He would have to pull himself about on some sort of wheeled board . . . but here in a mining town where all the streets were dirt and the sidewalks were rough board? And did not conscience demand that he consult the patient himself before the operation? He knew, Dr. Hart did, that total anesthesia was impossible with chloroform. There would come screams of agony if he did not put his patilent completely under.

The doctor again fell into a drowse, only to awaken when he heard his assistant supplying chloroform to the nostrils of the dying man. The stench of gangrene was oppressive and fully in evidence. "Andy, my hammer and chisel." The assistant promptly produced the instruments within ten to fifteen minutes. Hart had removed the plaster casts from both legs and tossed them into a pile of debris outside an open window.

"Tie down both wrists, Andy." The assistant followed the order, after which the doctor, taking a hefty swallow of whiskey, proceeded to cut into the flesh of the first leg, completely circling the limb when Hart called for suture thread. The assistant, his hands bloodied completely, managed to tie the thread around the artery and snipped the thread with scissors. The procedure for the second leg was the same. The assistant kept feeding the chloroform into the patient's nostrils amid loud cries, more like screams, and intense shouts of pain as the doctor continued the double amputation under the stress of unimaginable pain both to himself as the surgeon and to the patient losing his legs.

Surgeon Hart cut to the bone. Using the crude saw, he severed the thigh bones and Andy scissoring the remaining flesh. Hart handed each leg to his assistant, who like the casts pitched the severed limbs out the open window onto a pile outside. Andy hastily snatched clean sheets, handing them to the doctor, who stipped away the bloodied sheets while And held the patient in his arms.

"Don't let up, Andy." Hart took another two hefty swallows of whiskey from a bottle on the side stand. Andy did the same.

"I have nothing for the man's pain . . . nothing . . . nothing." Hart sat down in his chair, exhausted by the ordeal, his hands covered with blood, and visibly moved, tears in his eyes and on his cheeks. Cutting off a man's legs was the hardest surgery he had ever performed.

"How long, Doctor?"

"Let's see if he can sleep. I'm right here." The doctor poured whiskey over each stump and rewrapped the amputated limbs with more gauze. The task consumed almost his total supply. The clock on the shelf behind the surgery table ticked on marking the patient's moans. It was dawning in the east. The crags were invisible in clouds. The town of Calico and surrounding lowlands and the lake began to take on greens and orange-yellows and granite rocks of gray on the distance slopes.

"I think he is sleeping, Dr. Hart."

"I hope to God he is. If you can pray, pray for him and for me as well, Andy."

"I will try, sir." The assistant bowed his head in silent prayer.

Hart knew not what amount of time had passed. Andy had gone into another room to catch a rocky, shallow hour of rest, and Dr. Hart had fallen asleep. After washing the blood from his hands in a side basin, his head at last rested on the bed headboard. He was awakened by a great outcry of pain, the anguish of discovery in its deepest sense.

"My legs! They're gone. Oh, God, God help me. My legs!" He tried to lift up from the pillow to see better. "They're gone . . . my legs are missing! Oh, God!" he cried aloud, his voice reaching some early awakened citizens of the community. "You cut off my legs, Doctor . . . Doctor . . . Doctor!"

"I'm here."

"You cut off my legs. Goddamn you to everlastin' hell. You cut off my legs . . . they're gone!"

"You would have died . . . they were infected . . . they would have killed you . . . without a chance for your survival."

"Oh, God!" The patient sank into a whimper, crying openly and murmuring, "My legs . . . my legs . . . they're gone."

"You're alive, Tonny. That's what's important."

"You're a goddamn liar! My legs are what are important."

"Those infected legs—they would have caused your death in three days. We'll work something out." The doctor filled a glass of whiskey, what remained after his and Andy's doses. "How about a tumbler of whiskey. We got plenty of that." Hart finished pouring a tumbler of whiskey for his patient. His arm under the man's head, he let the patient sip, slowly emptying the contents of the glass. He lay the patient's head back down onto the pillow, still bleeding from the stumps yet lucky to be alive. The patient fell asleep.

"Andy!" he called. The assistant appeared in the doorway to the operating room.

"I was just getting some rest." He had buried the debris.

"I understand. When he falls asleep, see if you can change his sheets."

"I'll do it. sir."

"The whiskey will help. You're a good man, Andy."

He described the shitless and bare-bodied miners, sweating even in the year-round cool of the mine, as the metallic strikes of their picks and abrasive working of their shovels to uncover new deposits of silver mixed with turquoise. The men were, in fact, boys of teen age, some of them, worked alongside miners who had come to the mine from other countries, England first. Duval described amid the dust the crazy, criss-crossing working tangle of light beams from the miners' lanterns affixed on the helmets. Their labor appeared endless yet productive as they loaded the ore carts that stood on rails to one side of the tunnel. He described the sweaty bodied and a sense of the presence of the mountain, as a powerful force that hovered over their every effort as their shovels clanged and scraped, their wedge bars clanged and pics struck into the black ground of the mountain's core. No words passed between the men while they worked. From time to time, a miner would spit out dust he had sucked in through his bearded open mouth. Then, again, a miner would lay down his tool to rest. To Duval's eyes, as reporter to the paper's readers, it appeared that the scene of work in the silver mine was endless, without rest or slack. The miners picked and shoveled as they devoured nature's provision.

Duval described the collapse of the tunnel, a catastrophe caused by inadequate shoring in the mine roof in a place where no rock gave natural support. He then went into details about the sudden fall out of the rock and the entrapment of a thirty-year-old miner named Tommy. That was all he knew about the man. Both legs had been trapped by the rock fall, and it took four men with pry bars and shovels to free him. The trapped victim was fortunate that the fall out had not totally covered him, crushing his chest. The poor fellow now lay in a bed at the cottage hospital of Dr. David Hart.

Duval finished his story at around midnight. He threw himself across the unopened bed and was soon asleep with exhaustion. The oil burned low in his table lantern.

When he awoke at daybreak, Duval poured some water from a pitcher and washed his face in a basin provided by the hotel. He clumped down the hotel stairs and out into the morning's frigid air. He set off for a bowl of hot porridge at the Sasparilla cafe and grill up a short distance on Miner Street. He walked slowly, breathing in the deep saturation of fresh morning air that always revealed the wintry wealther atop the crag rising fifteen thousand feet above the village of Calico. Now and then he let the slight wafting of frozen air from off the summit snows of the Sierras. Winter was approaching. It would arrive earlier, he surmised, depending on the storm front movement of cold air—earlier than it arrived at lower elevations.

He entered the Lackadaisy Cafe—a Sasparilla stop for nondrinkers in a village already marked with seven taverns. At the counter he ordered hot cereal, this time oatmeal with fresh milk and a cup of steaming coffee. He ate verress was a a male—the only woman he had seen was the mother strolling with her baby the day he rescued them both from death. He had heard idle talk in the mine that prostitutes were headed his way, Calico giving them promise of instant riches. Yet since that day no female had appeared on the street of this mining town at the foot of the High Sierras. Since carpenters had begun to build a one-room schoolhouse not far away from Miner Street, it was obvious to any observer that Calico wanted, expected, and was preparing for families to move into Calico. They did so at their own risk. Shootings at a tavern were commonplace; there were, to his knowledge, no gun laws to control such eruptions of deadly range at a tavern . . . or for that matter, anywhere on a street. Calico's isolation behind the Sierras seemed to invite outlaws of the worst sort, silence they felt protected by the mountains from the law west of the Sierras. On this particular morning, Duval, his story in his pocket, was one of the early observers of the growing contempt for law and the violence it invited. Life was cheap in Calico.

On the morning after the accident and before his reporter had turned in his story, newspaper editor Dixon and his wife Edna had risen for the day and were enjoying their breakfast in their small cottage on the outskirts of Calico when Duval dropped off his report at their house, not expecting them to be up yet.

Greetings at the door were informal. When Duval handed his story to the editor, Dixon said a low "Good morning, Duval." He read the first few lines of the story and responded, "Readers will get a picture of what happens down in a mine when the timber shoring gives way."

"That should be exciting."

"Come in, come in. Don't just stand there. Had breakfast.?"

"At the Lackadaisy Cafe, sir."

"Good. A reporter should always start out his day sober, if you know what I mean."

"I think I do, Mr. Dixon. Accuracy is important."

"Just so. Edna, here's my best reporter. Mr. Duval . . . Bruce is it?" Duval nodded. "Met my wife Edna . . . this is Mr. Duval, reporter and, I might add, a man experienced in rescue work. Sit down, sit down, Duval."

"Pleased to meet you, Mr. Duval. I overheard . . . you've had breakfast? You wouldn't turn down a hot cup of coffee?"

"No, ma'am," the reporter replied.

"What do you think of him, Edna? He's been here in our home not twenty minutes. Does Duval appear in any way . . . strange to you?" Duval grew extremely uncomfortable that Dixon should be appraising him as if he did not stand in his presence. "Well . . . like he is hiding something, trying to escape a . . . a bad situation? Do you think he is all that he pretends to be . . . or confesses to . . . ? That story in your hand will reveal the man, dear."

"I don't know exactly what you mean, Henry. He's too clean-cut a a man to be a fugitive or a . . . ."

"Man with a past."

"I didn't say that, Henry."

"Well, let's let the subject go. We can take him for his visible qualities. That's good enough for any man."

"I'll pass that offer of hot coffee, ma'am. I came here to drop off my story of a mine accident for the paper. I did not come here to be humiliated, a man with a past, indeed. We all have pasts of one sort of another."

"He's right. You see, Duval, we here in Calico have become unnerved by events of the past few months . . . shootings, one suicide, escapees from various jails and prison camps . . . all in the quest for silver. Forgive me, Duval. That was simply a test of character. Yours is sterling, no pun intended. And my dear Edna here, she sometimes drifts away from anchor, but it helps me to sort out the phonies from the real stock-in-trade reporter. I hope you understand, Mr. Duval."

"I think I can take it, sir. My story will bring more readers to your paper, I'm sure."

"I have special assignment for you, Duval. Seven tavern have opened up here in Calico. They are the source of revenue for their owners, of course, but they are also dens of rage and gun play. We've had three, four shootings the past month in two of the taverns. Go . . . visit each and get the story of reasons for these senseless murders. Don't expect to find reasons. Is it suspicion, jealous rage, robbery gone afoul for one reason or another . . . and who, if you can identify them . . . who are these shooters? What have the tavern owners done to end this stupid gunfire and its toll of murders. Get as many facts as you can, Duval. If you can find a vest of armor somewhere, better put it on but let me caution you, take no firearm with you. Instead, be slippery, subtle, and dumb . . . and as undetectable as a spider in his web. Un'erstand?"

"Gotcha. This may take me a while . . . say two weeks."

"Two months . . . whatever it takes . . . but get the story, and I'll print it. I could be shot at any time, as you damn well know."

"I shall keep these things in mind, sir."

"No coffee, Mr. Duval?" Edna asked.

"No, I think not. I'll get right on the story."

The editor gave his reporter a weak salututation with one hand and opened the front door for him. and Duval was gone to the Archive Tavern on Fiske Street, the same street the casino and the miners' rooming house were on.

Editor Dixon had not mentioned any tavern in particular, and because Duval had seen this tavern's opening day while on a visit to the miners rooming house, he would visit the Archive Tavern first.

It was eight in the morning. Under ordinary circumstances a tavern would be empty of customers at this hour in the morning. Not so this time. The bar was jammed and the few tables occupied with card players. A number of guests were milling about on the floor. In short, the tavern was jammed with visitors, drinkers, and more than likely, a pickpocket or two and troublemakers. Duval stepped to the bar and reaching between two customers ordered a wine tonic, placing his dollar on the bar. The bartender gave him a sharp look and promptly served Duval the wine cooler. He was not a drinker, and furthermore, he needed to keep his wits about him. He sidled over to the card players, stopping at a table where the four men, miners off-shift, had placed silver coins, one bag of dust, gold, or silver, at his right hand.

A king and a queen called a four of spades. The man with the weaker hand was angered, not so much because of the superior hand as the manner in which the holder had called the lesser hand. An argument broke out, and there before Duval's astonished hands, the holder of the four of spades pulled out a pistol and, pointing it at the other man who sat across the table from him, demanded that the high-hand reveal his entire hand. The pistol wavered in the hand of the holder.

"You can't make me lay down my cards, not with that pistol pointing to my face."

"I can't, eh." With that reply, the man with the gun shot into the ceiling to prove his mettle. The bartender hastened over and ordered the man with the gun to put it away before anybody got hurt.

"This yer chimp wants to hurry my hand, and I ain't about to get in no hurry."

"Pet yer gun away, mister. This is here's a card game only. You don't want to get into any trouble by killin' a man over a stupid game of cards."

"Maybe not way you see it. He's a tricky fellow, and I ain't about to put up with no crap from him."

"Put your gun away, mister," the bartender ordered, stepping out of the line of fire.

"Wal, jes to show you I mean business . . . there." He fired a round this time hitting his card-playing opponent in the shoulder. The man fell backward against the chair and slapped one hand to his wound. He ripped up his side of the table, spilling the coins of the other players and dumping the entire table onto the gun wielder. This move took everybody by surprise. The man wounded in the shoulder wove his way through the spectators, who had begun to regather on the floor of the room, the gunshot having sent them in all directions. Duval, witness to the scene, had his story. Going over to the bar, Duval put his glass on the counter, having taken only a couple of sips. He exited the tavern. He did not know the entire story, but the true cause for the deadly flareup between the card players, but the evidence of a willingness of a potential murderer to shoot it out because of an argument over cards argument was readily obvious.

The Silver Queen was the next tavern and, he hoped, the last, thinking that Dixon should be, or would be, satisfied with his stories about the two watering holes in Calico. Guns were everywhere. Miners, and they were the largest percentage by far of the town's population, carried them in curious ways. Occasionally a miner, wearing his own and not the mine's helmet, carried a small derringer revolver in the band of the helmet. Other times, Duval had spotted pistols in the straps of a man's boot and in his waistband.

Arguments on the street had already proven deadly. At the Silver Queen, over on Pine Street in the middle of the town, he found this tavern. He noted a horse tied at the hitching rail in front of the porch. Like the Archive Tavern, this place was filled with off-shift miners. His approach was the same. He stepped up to the crowded bar and ordered a whiskey tonic, which he deliberately spilled on his shirt as he bumped across the room, in the same manner sitting at the card tables, the usual centers of violent assault and debate over cards. There appeared, to his surprise, a male dressed in red satin like a lady of fashion, and well-bosomed, wearing a blonde wig and lipstick. To his added surprise, a guitarist strummed up from a chair in one corner, whereupon the gilded transvestite began to sing "Cuddle Up a Little Closer," fitting crowded midmorning tavern clientele. Weak applause followed the wigged blonde's rendition of a new hit, as it were. He sang "Waiting for the Robert E. Lee" as an encore performance, the applause not being quite deafening but audible. Duval always came onto the scene when other action common to tavern life had preceded the outbreak of violence. This time, it was the blonde transvestite who, having presented the crowd tavern with music engaged in an argument with a burly miner who took offense as the male caricature of a lady of fashion. The very presence of the singer and the suggestion by a deviate of any sort of familiar closeness enfuriated the burly chap who standing abruptly from his table, where he had sat drinking, not a card player this time, walked over to the slugger and pasted him across the face several times with a heavy hand.

The singer threw off his blond wig, and they got into it. The crowd backed away to watch the battle as the manager, this time not the bartender, pushed his guests aside with both arms and stepped in between the two men.

"Sit down . . . the both of you. This ain't no place for a fistfight. You can finish it off later," he dared to say, "out in the street. Meantime, I'm servilng each of you a drink of your choice providing you do no more fighting in the Silver Queen." The combatants were silent, until the de-wigged lady ordered a straight beer and the burly chap who was offended ordered a whiskey.

"You two guys separate. I don't want to see you anywhere close to each other, okay? This is a peace tavern. I got to be careful of my reputation. You understand."

The combatants were silent. The bartender served each man his drink. Duval found this an entertaining story and planned to write it in detail. But the fight was not over. Liquored up, the burly miner, unknown to the manager, had sported a revolver in the tavern. Seeing his opponent through the crowd, he pulled the revolver and deliberately murdered the transvestite in the blonde wig, discarded before the fight. He murdered the female impersonator tethered at the rail then fled out the door and, leaping on a horse, galloped away down Pine Street in the direction of the mill and the row of prostitution houses. At least a dozen guests of the Silver Queen had seen the action and would be willing witnesses at any trial. The problem was that in Calico, there were neither gun control laws nor any sense of the value of human life. Duval knew these things. It was just the sort of primitive western town, isolated, strategically hidden, behind the mountains, a retreat for murderers, thugs, robbers, and stagecoach bandits. All of this riffraff had made themselves visible in the brief history of the silver lining town. This was one of the more glaring murders and would last long in the memories of the miners who had witnessed the shooting. Such was the knowledge of Duval, reporter for the the only newspaper. His scarcely took a sniff of the whiskey sour, deliberately spilling it on his vest with the knock of a stranger's elbow. He was determined to remain sober. He stopped in at the Sasparilla grill where he ordered a cheese sandwich and a glass of milk. He returned to his room at the International Hotel to write his story for the paper. In his mind was the power of words. He would emphasize the nature of the crime he had witnessed . . . the ruthlessness of the murder.

In the Dixon home, while Duval was scribbling his news stories of his visits to two of Calico's liveliest taverns, as the news editor called them, the paper's editor and his wife were discussing their one, lone reporter. Dixon felt somewhat responsible for inviting any other men so talented as Duval to join the news team. Calico was a dangerous town to dwell in, much more to wander the streets in search of news. For those reasons, the editor was content with giving Duval direct assignments, the very fact of exposure on the streets was in itself a danger to a man's personal safety.

"Keep him. He's a good reporter."

"He is . . . conscientious."

"Good reaper of the facts . . . young, energetic."

"I will keep him. He asks no special privileges, that's what I like. He's aggressive like a tiger."

"Good, That's why he's a good reporter. We've got to keep people interested in the *Eagle*. When a story sounds like a political report from Sacramento, we lose readers."

"Nothing wrong with politics as such, is there, Andy?"

"No, not until they grow unduly opinionated . . . smear one another. dump the opponent into the tar pit."

"Well, a good political fight is newsworthy."

"Duval is on a scene where the action is, I can say that for him." Dixon's usual placid manner changed to one of indignation. He had his ideas about individual merit, value-seeking righteous swell-heads, dabblers in the luxury of changeable ethics.

"Being a truth-seeker is better than being a collaborator or a saboteur or a a . . . malcontent or . . . a . . . ." He ran out of dark ministers of justice.

"Maybe we can ask the seer. Have you forgotten? I've already invited half a dozen people to our night with a magician, a worker of magic and a . . . a practitioner of the mysticism of a seance. You know how folks go for that sort of entertainment. They like to be puzzled."

"All of that at one time?"

"Why not, Andy? Small-town life is such a bore for some folks. A few women have moved to Calico, I've learned . . . and not just the illicit sort. That's probably news to you. The town needs brightening once in a while."

"We shall see, Mrs. Dixon." She returned to her V Andy Dixon ictorian chores at the great hearth over which hung the hanging fruit, berries, herbs. She was lucky to have such a hearth in a village where a wood-burning stove was the mark of village home comfort. Some masons were rare in Calico. Most working men preferred the mine to the construction of primitive, windswept cottage construction. Andy Dixon had managed to furnish their house with handcarved chairs and dining room table, with shelves that glistened with delicate blue and gold chinaware. A tall grandfather clock stood in one corner of their living room. Haning from carved wooden forest branches on one was an elegant Victorian mug table. Candle wall sconces supplied the only nighttime light in the main room of the cottage. A handmade carpet of flowers, reeds design and of and rock-gray color covered the living room floor. Over the course of a year and a half, Mr. Dixon had wagoned hese essential furnishings from depots in San Francisco. He was a very resourceful man, as his newspaper the *Eagle* also attests to this practical virtue, common among early settlers in Calico and elsewhere in the country. The residents of Calico were no less resourceful. Mrs. Dixon was preparing fruit turnovers, beer, and coffee for their guests. A very clever woman, she had learned how to make potato beer by an old-country recipe.

Dixon took a seat in their one upholstered, stuff-backed armchair and studied the proof page from his newspaper press. The thought suddenly occurred to him: what if this seer proved to be a fake. Then again, what if he demonstrated the truth of such absolutes as love, mercy, compromise, temptation? His mind drifted off into a silent analysis of the word *truth*. How that any collection of facts about reality demonstrate a truth instead of an observation of change or an opinion? Facts changed . . . thus truth about those facts changed. No? Or was that changing truth merely an opinion or an illusion of permanence? If opinions were truths, then there was no absolute truth. Opinion all too often bore the weight of feelings and feelings had the capacity to misinform and to deceive. Dixon came to that conclusion in his easy chair. He was not alone in this vein of thinking for the enlightment of resonant logic had worked for decades to overturn traditional values and personal confidence in them as guides in life. Men were left to grapple with the invisible and struggle against the blasphemy of a doctrine that appeared to resemble a value. He felt that he was getting into deep waters.

Dixon spoke aloud his thoughts to his wife and the hearth, who was busy with the preparation of the berry turnovers. "I didn't know Calico needs a seer,"

She straightened up and turned toward him. "Oh, yes. Every growing town needs a professional seer."

"A professional seer . . . hmm. What is the name of our visiting . . . seer?"

"I think his name is . . . is . . . Tabor Mohammud. I'm not quite sure. I'm told he has hade his presence known in Europe."

"A European seer! Great Scott! What more could we ask for? That a European seer should bend so low as to come to the village of Calico! Incredible!"

"Now, dear, we must not make fun of him, please. He's a very sensitive man and, besides, it's not every day that we have the opportunity to entertain a genuine European seer in our midst."

"Entertain, I dare say."

"Well, we must treat him right . . . no sarcasm, please, Andy. Such opportunities come only once in a lifetime."

He mumbled, "Opportunities . . ."

"I've personally invited him . . . to come here, meet my guests and perhaps tell one or two fortunes. It isn't often we can look into the future. Let's see what Mr. Muhammud has to say about our star reporter." Dixon smiled to himself, receiving back from the hearth only silence . . . and wonder on the part of his wife.

"Duval is no star, Edna. Maybe this Mr. Mohammud can enlighten me on how to run a newspaper . . . for profit."

"Oh, dear, profit again!"

"Exactly. Perhaps, just maybe he can tell us a little more about Duval, a reporter for the *Eagle*. Well, I won't enter his remarks into the paper or into Mr. Duval's work record. I tell you, privately. I have heard that he killed a man in San Francisco . . . or at least put the man in a hospital. That would make Mr. Duval a fugitive . . . ." Silence ensued from the hearth except for thertle of the tin pie pan. Dixon retreated into himself again and wrestled with the question of truth . . . truth as an absolute . . . or was it slimly a figment of the intellectual imagination or an idea to be debated? If a mystic make truth appear to be absolute yet change its nature into a value that is bendable, flexible, then the only truth is the truth that an absolute does not exist. We are then free to devise truths that others will accept . . . opinions, in fact, labelled as "truths." Life becomes thereby easier, in a way, until one's convictions are challenged by an opinion said to be a truth. The illusion of absolutes thus disappears; in its place, why, a man can insert an opinion that has the stature of a truth. Are not laws therefore disguised opinions that are championed as truth?

Dixon did not finish his search for an absolute when there came a knock with the brass knocker on the front door. Mrs. Dixon, taper in hand, walked about the living room lighting the candles in the wall sconces. She stopped in her chore and motioned with her head for her husband to respond to the knock.

He thought the knock was the first of their guests. Instead, it was the pressman, who handed Dixon a sheet that contained the corrections he had penciled into the first proof page. Dixon was a perfectionist in this matter of correct readability, a well-proofed newspaper marking a well-situated editor. The pressman departed, and Dixon closed the door, walking to a buffet where he placed the news sheet.

"He has no family. I should have invited the man . . . his name's Bruce . . . I should have invited him to our seance."

"Next time. Back to my reporter, he's single . . . has a girl-friend . . . fiancee. I don't know. Mentions her from time to time."

"Girlfriend . . . his fiancee . . . in San Francisco?"

"If he did some damage to another man in the city . . . let the law take care of it. For now, he's a damned good reporter. They don't know for certain . . . the police, the sheriff, I mean."

"I wouldn't think any more about it . . . 'ts speculation."

"I don't know, Edna. Right now . . . just a rumor. I don't know where I heard it."

A flaw in editor Dixon's character was his capacity for voicing and making public half-truths, on the assumption that the listener or the reader of the *Eagle* would fill in the other half or missing links of the story. This capacity to censor the truth was not evident in a village newspaper where gossip was news and news was often hearsay. In a major big-city newspaper, any half-truth could have profound political consequences.

Editon Dixon had planned a special event for his invited guests on a cool March evening. Here in his town home, he need only announce their seer guest as a man of psychedelic insight and mystifying fortune-telling accuracy. The very mystery of who he was would increase the curiosity of Dixon's guests. Such is often the case in a dangerous world in which common folk look for leaders, preferring fantasy to reality in leadership. Thus, on this particular night with a room full of invited guests, they would be content, with no surprises and not a little frightened by the seer's prognostications. Indeed, the more withdrawn of Dixon's guests might even relish the seer's foreboding announcement of . . . of danger in Calico.

The Dixons' living and dining room furnishings, small and essential as they were, constituted a scene of shining hospitality. Candle flames lit the frosted-glass wall sconces and tall blue candlestick on the oak wall panels. All these unsteady flames cast a glow upon the carved legs of the polished mahogany table. The guests, chatting amiably among themselves and conscious of the excitement of the occasion, were the leaders in Calico—the banker, tradesmen, hotel manager, and Duval himself as a special guest of his editor, Frank Dixon. They had gathered by cordial and personal invitation to hear mystic figures popular in small towns, that lacked any other form of entertainment except bar fights, gang assaults, and stagecoach holdups. These diversions were scarcely enough to excite the imagination in a people visited by a plague of ongoing violence. A mystic, a seer, an afficionado of the occult was sure to provide the necessary relief from gunfire as well as entertain convivial guests as they reveled in their incredulity. A small-town seer came to town as much as for uplift as for entertainment and refreshing astonishment . . . almost like a religious convention.

Dr. Hart in his black vest suit with the gold watch chain looked especially bright with enthusiasm. He had the habit of pulling at his pointed beard and checking his watch, as if he were counting the pulse of the Dixon guests. He had seen death and was curious to examine its personality, presented by a mystic. Mr. Combs, the only banker in Calico, had no wife. He came with his hound dog on a short leash. Perhaps even a banker could learn a thing or two about hidden investments. His ruddy face and shock of when hair made him an eager witness to mysticism. The year before, anger had shone in his blue eyes over the mystical disappearance of a depositor's funds in his bank. His habit was to continually pull up on his trousers, showing his gartered stockings. Like the doctor, he was nattily dressed. The gunsmith arrived by horseback, attired in a shirt of leather dungarees and jacket. As expected, he wore a brace of pistols and kept looking askance, as if he sustected stalkers with bad intentions. Small of stature, he fit nicely into the one cushioned chair in the living room. The smithy arrived natilly attired in leather. Strange to behold, he carried across his back a crossbow that he had fashioned at his forge and that he wanted to show Editor Dixon in the hope for a little publicity that might turn into a lucrative trade, apart from barrel hoops, wagon rims, hand tools such as mallets and axe heads.

Mr. Taylor, the dry goods man, apologizrf for his tardiness in a fine linen suit with embroidered button loops and epaulets as life here a military figure. He had served the town well and need not apologize for his attire. His dark eyes shone through his swarthy complexion. They serviced smiles that he practices on his customers at his general store where pickles and topcoats marked the lines of goods at his disposal for sale. A woman crept into the gathering, newly arrived in Calico and set up for business in what would become known as the red light district. She wore a fur wrap and red gown as if this were a wedding reception. Mr. Dixon wanted the female expression, the wonderment from a lady such as she who plied her trade in the realm of the mystical. Who were the men who came to her for relief, were the apparitions . . . ghosts of past fatherhood, wonders of male vigor and participators in community life? Or were they simply outcasts? In any event, here she was, gorgeous of figure and well-dressed as one have expected. She was a blonde with blue eyes. Dixon greeted her with cordial indifference, as he did with his other guests.

A minister, portly with freshly shaven cheeks. Crimson suspenders supported trousers with a knifelike crease. He arrived without a coat, keen of mind to enquire about the occult, perhaps to add a warning to his Sunday worshippers about the devil's alliances, spiritual of a sort but from a world of darkness. The last guest to arrive, other than Duval, was a lawyer . . . as one might have expected in an outlaw town . . . although his arrival was without incident or surprise. He had migrated to Calico to mitigate the pain of those who had been shot, robbed, and raped of their ordinary human happiness by marauders of one sort or another. Silver in abundance was his expected reward for these services. Silver was Calico's birthright, and there they were. When Duval arrived, in knickers and warmed by a woolen jacket of undefinable yellowish hue, Dixon seated him on a dining room chair to observe and record, for the paper, the advent of mysticism into Calico, a town where even the present location of silver had its mysteries.

They were the common folks of Calico, the druggist, a Mr. Harrison who came with the druggist insignia emblazoned on a frock coat. He was alone, a small spindly figure of a man. The sawmill owner, Francils Duggan, arrived alone, he in an embroidered shirt and dungarees, a powerful man with muscles that bulged beneath his maroon sweater, a smile of ingratiation fixed on his face. A lawyer named Princep Gustaffson arrived on horseback, his polished boots catching the shine of the candlelight on his balding head. The owner of the Empire Mine had apparently walked to the Dixon cottage for he was in a mild sweat when he arrived. He was a dark-skinned man wh a fine moustache and quick eyes that glanced about the room. And then, of course, there was the small energetic figure of the host himself, his black hair combed back and his black horn-rimmed glasses fixed atop his long nose. The lovely Edna Dixon her graying hair fixed in a bun with a comb went about the room greeting all in friendly banter and with a handshake, occasionally asking how they liked living in Calico.

"You folks just make yourselves comfortable. We have a special guest tonight, a man who's a stranger to Calico, a seer and a hypnotist. Meantime, I invite you to the dining room table for cakes and coffee. Please partake and let the party begin." This cordial invitation put the roomful of guests into motion as they responded to their hostesses invitation beginning freely to converse among themselves. These guests of the Dixons were some of the leaders and backers in Calico. One of those guests who may or may not have been invited was the sheriff of the counthy. Dixon was quick to usher him into his home with a careless aplomb as just another guest. The sheriff had appeared suddenly and unexpectedly. Duval's face assumed an aspect of fear and flight, but he kept his calm. Duval had entered early and found a place in the shadows of one corner. The sheriff looked about the room and seeing the reporter huddled in stony inactivity, steeling himself for the unexpected. Innocent though he was, he knew the purpose of the sheriff's visit, to remain as small and unnoticeable as possible.

"When the party is over, Duval, I have a wagon outside. I would like to take you to he station for questioning. The man is a celebrity, folks. I know you are innocent, Duval, but I have questions about . . . that night . . . I want to ask . . . if you would be so kind."

"Sure, why not, Sheriff. Do the Dixons know you're here . . . on business?"

"I'm just a visitor . . . I like to get acquainted with folks here in Calico."

"I imagine you do . . . what with all the shootings of late. Do you follow the gangs . . . I mean the punks from 'Frisco, haven for gunfighters. You know what I man." The sheriff was silent.

Mrs. Dixon's guests were very loquacious. They nodded, chatted loudly, hardly taking notice of the sheriff and his conversation with Duval. They regarded the strange duo as a part of the invitee townsmen, sheriff included. The sheriff did not sport a badage at this time. They laughed loudly and looked about as if expecting other guests. They watched their hostess arrange plates of sweetbread and cookies and petite sandwiches on the dining room table. This was more of a social event than a party with a mysterious entertainer, a seer and mystic for a special man of fame. object of her announcement that Monsieur Muhammud will entertain us shortly. Meanwhile . . . enjoy yurselves." A few more moments of convivial banter transpired before Mrs. Dixon, taking the center of the small room, again clapped her hands to gather their full attention and silence.

"And now, my friends and neighbors of Calico, may I present our entertaining maestro and famed and world-eknowned visitor for the evening, Mr. Jabsel Muhammud, seer and ventriloquist of international reputation." The Dixon guests applauded with enthusiasm and keen attention, looking about for the appearance of the great one.

A small figure of a man, attired in a black velvet suit with parted gray hair and displaying a full beard well groomed, stepped to the center of the room. The guests fidgeted quietly with surprise. They were eager to watch and become involved. They had had enough of gang warfare. They were eager to be entertained.

"Greetings, ladies and gentlemen. It is a distinct pleasure for me to visit with you this evenin' and to ride in my buggy through your beautiful town of Calico." Applause followed these brief remarks. Mrs. Dixon smiled; her husband looked pleased. "First, let me say that I possess as well the powers of divination and hypnotic energy . . . and gravitational defiance," The seer spoke with a foreign accent, French or Latin, one had to guess. "Madam," he said to Mrs. Dixon, "if you would lower the light, I shall raise this coffee table to a height of six inches off the floor . . . providing you all close your eyes in order for me to perform the magic some have called it." Edna snuffed out three of the wall sconces, and the guests closed their eyes.

"You open your eyes." To the guests' amazement, the coffee table had risen half a foot. There were faint curses of astonishment. Several of them shook their heads in disbelief.

"Shut your eyes again." The women looked sheepishly at the men who grimaced, and one of the skeptics smiled. They followed the seer's instructions. They obeyed his command and when invited to do so, opening them again only to observe that the table had resumed its customary place before the sofa, in front of the expressions of amazement on the faces of Dixons' guests. "You all have come here not to observe an act of magic performed, but to learn what lies head for our lovely little town of Calico." The guests were silent. The seer spoke, "I can express my vision in one word . . . trouble in Calico. The atmosphere of the town will become violent." The guests gave a strange and erupting outcry of alarm and resentment, emitting gasps of surprise and disbelief as if suddenly released from death and bloodshed and some ominous sense of catastrophic destruction. The guests looked at one another as if strangers; here and there came a murmur of disquiet. They knew that the immorality of danger was the existence and evidence of irresponsibility for the cause of danger and risk everyday in Calico. Their host reflected to himself that the only ethic involved in acts of violence was the ethic of choice of victims. That had ideological sosurces. The morality came in the escape from that irresponsibility of causing an act of violence.

"I manage a risky business in more ways than one," said banker, who had already experienced one failed holdup. Several others of the guests responded in pained expressions of denial. Where did this man get his foreknowledge? "He's spooky," said the storekeeper, regarding the smithy with a slight sneer.

"I can say no more. I do not want to shock or frighten you. You Americans take risks, but you do not always expect your fears. They come upon you like swarms of locusts. N'est-ce pas? These events will follow naturally . . . naturally." The seer looked about him, regarding each expression with a cynical curl of his lip. "Your town sheriff is capable of handling the events, I am certain. And now that I have entertained you all in my small way, I shall leave you with this prophesy. A powerful leader will assume command of your town of Calico. Follow him and beware!"

"May Zeus and Allah bless you abundantly." Mrs. Dixon invited him to her side with a beckoning finger.

"I speak for Muhammud. He dwells among the infinite. His vision is secure with the ages. He speaks the truth. This year and the next years promises to be filled with the excitement of a flourishing silver mining town." She broke off the overture to the future, and turning to her guests, she began to share some of the goodies on the table, as the guests entered into conversation with one another. One by one they wished the best for their guest seer, who shook their hands with a look of grim satisfaction. Then he, the invited seer, began to acknowledge their wealth and township and prosperity by voicing prophetic future scenes of violence and disaster for Calico. He began, thus, in a voice that seemed to have been dipped in poisonous syrup: "Friends of the future . . . ghosts . . . for ye are all ghosts in my vision of Calico. This town will experience rape, not by invaders, but by the greed of the hungry entrepreneurs of Silver Town. The bank will go broke, bankrupt not by the immensity of its silver deposits but by it investments in worthless land, the buyers of which never appear to make their payments. There will come a time of famine, during which wagons will be sent to San Francisco and to neighboring towns to obtain food for the starving citizens of Calico. You will know sickness and disease, imported by aliens to Calico, who will spread killers . . . no medical help . . . that will exterminate almost one-third of the people who live here, including the children. The pride you take in your schools will become empty and poisonous. It will lead to their ignorance instead of knowledge. There will spring up flames of fire that are extinguished only by the patriots of Calico, but fire from your drug habits and your smoking will at times ravage parts of the town, only in the end after twenty years of prosperity seeking, the entire town will be consumed in a massive sweep of flames. You will pray to your god, but he will not hear you because your god is the god of the faithful. He is not the god of the Philistines. My powers as a seer are incontrovertible. You take me for a foreigner and entertainer. I am both; and I am also an extinguisher of beauty, life and wealth. I do not prophesy in futility."

At this moment Mr. Dixon stepped to the center of the room and began to try to disparage and to cancel the dark and destructive words of the seer on the guests. Several of them moved, stood, and prepared to depart the scene, which had grown uncomfortable for all. They were especially offended by the seer's reference to them as "ghosts." The reporter, Duval, and the sheriff appeared equally distressed and ready to flee the scene of dissolute predictions depicted by the seer. The banker and the dry goods manager had briskly left the cottage, with gestures thanking the Dixons for their hospitality. Duval believed that he would have his chance for rebuttal in the editor's office of the *Eagle*.

He felt a hand on one arm and moved as directed. Duval and the sheriff climbed into what appeared to be a hearse, harnessed by two dapple grays, waiting, stomping, and snorting like fire horses. The sheriff, with Duval in handcuffs, set out toward the main part of the town. They had no soonerer arrived on the corner of Miner and Fiske than shots hammered out. The sheriff turned to Duval. "You're off the hook. I'm not done with; you." He removed the handcuffs from Duval's wrists. "We'll meet again. Get out!" Duval complied and the hearse wagon lurched, a deputy cranking the siren as it sped toward the location of the gunshots. Close to the new hotel of brick, the place where a gambling hall had been set up in the basement. The hand-cranked siren pealed through the street in the direction of the building. Duval could only guess the source of the gunshots. He was left to walk back to his hotel room. arriving, he immediately sat down and wrote his story about the injured miner, the crucial danger of more caveins in the silver mine. Finishing his story about the cave-in, he wrote a brief story about the guest seer at the Dixon home and alluded to his unfavorable leak and disastrous future of Calico, predictions about the town's future in the face of evidence to the contrary. Duval, the town's only reporter, walked to the newspaper office and dropped his two reports into the slot. He decided to walk to the brick hotel to investigate the gunshots.

A large crowd had gathered in front of the hotel. Among them are customers dressed for a night of good luck at the wheels and cards in the casino. Also, among them were miners in work dungarees, gaming-table masters in elastic shirtsleeves. Pushing through the crowd, Duval saw a body lying sprawled upon the ground in front of the hotel. The sheriff was inspecting items he had removed from the victim's pockets, his deputy having strung a rope from lamppost to hitching rail to keep the crowd back. The investigative process was slow.

The victim was killed by a shot to the head. That was obvious to the crowd as well.

Duval's disappearance on the night he remembered well. As a reporter in a small Sierra town, he wanted to make good in his profession as well as to marry his fiancee. The best solution, he concluded . . . as he reread her letter cautioning silence, was to gather together a cadre of four to six men who could follow instructions. They would visit the various businesses in Calico and . . . for a very small fee . . . in order to caution them against bandits, robbers in the town, malcontents, and roaming rogues who sought to kill and to plunder. Calico was a special target for such agents of violence. He put Vivian's letter away and sat down to reply to her words of caution

He sealed the envelope and took it down stairs where he handed it to Jere, the clerk at the desk. He would put his plan into operation in the morning, He had no assignment from the paper's editor, usually a note left in his box. An enterprising, small-town entrepreneur had constructed a rickety, hastily built boarding house for itinerant miners in the town. That badge included about 90 percent of the men working in the mine. They often slept at their boarding house in shifts. Two men worked the kitchen, preparing one meal and the lunch buckets. It was there Duval went the following day to begin to muster his small clique— he hesitated calling them "the mob" or "the gang" of enforcers—even though his plan involved a hint of threats and payoffs, which he would describe as protection pay or, in short, police work. He spent little time there, acquired a list of the fifty-four tenants. He made himself known to as many as he could find, telling them that he was mounting a police force to protect the citizens from gang violence. He represented himself as "the Management" then, he added, he was also a newspaperman who was helping the business owners to succeed. He said no more, merely suggesting that the town could use a mayor. This last suggestion was greeted by the miners with indifference. What had a mayor to do with mining silver? Nonetheless, of the new body of enforcers, he would be the management, as a newsman for the money. With this introduction and these few words, Duval left the building. He would need some sort of special clothing, a uniform, a consistency of appearance, for his mustered enforcers. clothes, those befitting a mayor godfather.

He had decided to combine the office of newsman with the action in the hyphenated signature—Dylan Duval, Mayor. He stopped by the press office arranged for a stamp and a business card, a calling card it was named, to indicate his new profession as a self-appointed mayor of Calico. At the outfitters, where other items such as leather vests, boots, and hunters caps and jackets were sold, he got outfitted with a fine business suit, for those occasions when he felt that either he should make a public appearance or call on one of his "constituents." All of his self-magnification was gaining a ready acceptance in his own mind, the details of which he was adding by the hour and the day, for he was in a second day of his "professional ascension.' He chuckled at the thought, his "term of office." *The devil be damned*, he thought.

Vivian would be proud of him in his new suit, and she would come to accept his new station as the mayor, protem, self-appointed, de facto of the small silver mining town of Calico, California. He strode from the general merchandise store of Calico with a pride that bordered on arrogance. He walked toward the office of the *Eagle*. When he opened the door and stepped inside, the editor gasped, his jaw fell, and he scanned his reporter from head to toe and back again.

*D*uval hammered on the font door to the boarding house. He struck twice, three times but received no sounds of a response within. He pressed the latch and walked in. Instinct told him the tenants miners on the second floor were at home. He rapped on the door. A mine ropened the door. He was tall, square shouldered, a hard face with a black beard and black eyes.

"Yes, yeah, whatssa matter."

"Can I come in and talk with you."

The miner swung the door wide open. When Duval stepped inside, he saw a second miner, a shorter man, just as rugged, wearing a blazer, his round face seathed in a full beard, his brown hair showing little care, hands like the tines of a small pitchfork. The voice of the first miner was hoarse, almost uteral. Both miners had so accommodated themselves in their one-room quarters that its untidy aspect was almost threatening. The second miner brought a candle to the door to examine their caller's face.

"Whatsa matter. You come with news."

Both miners were apparently single men or men who had left their families behind to go to the mines to dig for silver.

The miner put the candle on a table. He lit a second candle, letting the wax drip into a second saucer, set the lighted candle upright. He went to the window, one for the room, and stuffed a blanket into the racks around the windowpane. The miner found a chair for their untimely guest. Apparently these men had just finished their supper.

"My name is Duval. I'm looking for Calico residents who would take part in my plan to set up a police gang in Calico. The plan is very simple. Gangs have come down from San Francisco, and they have found Calico easy pickings. We need to protect our merchants and vendors here in this town. We have no police force. I am the mayor protem, that means temporary. I need some strong men who are willing to protect the residents, especially the merchants from these gangs of thieves who cross the mountains for no reason other than to rob the people of Calico. My plan is simple."

Duval looked toward the window, covered with a blanket. He regarded the features of the two miners who sat before him in the candlelight.

"The plan is simple. You protect the merchants. They give you a certain amount of money each time you call.

Protection money, like a security tax. I can use the money to start a school here in Calico. There are no children in the town, on the streets. The men of the town have been building a small schoolhouse over on the other side. You pay a visit every month to this merchant, that merchant, and you say to him, I will protect you from these gangs. They will not molest you if you will give us fifty dollars every month. That may seem like a lot of money to you . . . you tell the owner . . . but it will pay off in the protection we will give your store, your shop from these gangs who will rob and steal and commit other crimes. Do you understand what I am proposing to you?"

The two miners regarded each other with studied looks of doubt, skepticism, and wonder.

The second man with the full beard said, "Each merchant, every guy out there, we call on kicks in with fifty dollars when we call."

"That is the solution to crime in Calico."

The first man replied, "That's a sort of . . . protection racket in my opinion."

"These gangs . . . and I know of one and others will come because you have no protection."

The second man got up, went to a closet, and returned with a double-barreled shotgun.

This is our protection.

"I mean, sir, the shoekeepers."

"They got their guns fer protection."

"Won't work," said Duval. "Too slow. These bandits come armed, work fast, rob, and then disappear. There is one sheriff for the entire country."

The two men regarded each other again with quizzical expressions and doubt.

"What do we call ourselves."

"Soldiers of hell."

"Oh, and who knows us?"

"You will wear a jacket with the words, Hell's Vanguard. That . . . those words will warn the thieves that they are line for robuble."

"Well, I don' know," said the taller of the two men. He moved the two candles closer to their visitor. "Who do we call on?"

"The ferrier is a first, then the bootmaker, the market store manager, those three for starters."

"Do we keep any of the . . . swag?" the tall one asked.

"A parentage for your pay . . . if you do the job right."

"How will you know?"

"I will follow up, as your mayor, to see that all goes well. You will not work alone. I will find others to help in this matter. Our merchants in Calico need protection from gangs who swarm down from 'Frisco to rob us and they will not stop. As long as silver is mined from the mines, there will be money to bring them down here. That is inevitable."

"Where can we contact you, Mister . . . ?"

"Duval."

"Mr. Duval."

"At my hotel. Leave a note at the front desk. I'll pick it up."

The shorter of the two miners picked up a candle and walking to the front door opened it and waited for Duval to stand.

"Good to meet you men. 'Preciate your help. The job will pay more than digging in the mines."

"We gotta think about it," said the second miner with the full beard.

"Yeah, we'll let you know," said the first miner with the dark eyes, the man of tall, angular frame who held the door open. Duval stood, attempted to shake hands, but both men withheld their clasp. Duval exited the apartment and heard the door close behind him. It was a start.

As he tromped down the fish board steps of the boarding house, he snapped his fingers; he had for gotten to get their names. Oh, well, he thought, the tall one with the spiney voice and tattered jean was visible in his imagination, and the muscular weightlifting companion was equally as visible in recall. He would learn their names later.

When he stepped out of the doorway onto the boardwalk, he saw the lamplighter crew at work on one of the twenty lampposts recently installed along Fronstreet, about one hundred yards apart. They would make a good story for the *Eagle*.

The lamplighter was descending the fifteen foot ladder one careful step at a time. He held a smoking taper in one hand, the lighting wick that had lit the wick in a kerosene bowl within the globe at the top of the post. The lamplighting tool was nothing more than a common candle. On the ground there burned a lantern. A crew member stood beside the ladder to steady it. The lighter himself was a rough-faced man with a billed cap, working jeans, and jacket for wamth, with ratty boots marked by scratches and nicks, once black.

The lamplighter grabbed his lanterns by the bail. The other crew member seized the ladder, and lowering it, the two street lighters started for the next lamp. The man who carried the ladder swung along the boardwalk with a confident, strong stride, his field jacket flying as he walked, his crown woolen cap pulled down close to his eyes, for the cold drafts of air were beginning to flow down from the crags far above the town. When the pair of them reached the next lamplight, the procedure was the same. The ladder bearer positioned the ladder against the post below the dark glass bowl. The lamplighter pressed on the bail lever that raised the glass lamp cover, and placing the wick of his taper into the flame it the wicks, letting the glass slide hom ligth a light screech. As he was accustomed to doing, he carefully mounted the ladder, holding his taper in one hand and stopping halfway up to shield the flame from a rogue gust of crag summit wind. Continuing his ascent of the ladder while his companion held it steady, the lamplighter inserted his taper under the bowl, sosoted by the high flame of the burning lamplight and touched it to the wick. The flame caught readily. The lamplighter rolled the wick up high, causing it to smoke, knowing that by early morning the wick would have burned down to the latch and the flame would go out. At least half of the lights went out early in their sooted bowl, yet those remaining furnished passersby sufficient light to navigate the rough boardwalk that lined both sides of the main street in Calico. When Duval figured that he had his story and had asked for small vignettes from each man—one a family man of two girls, the other a single man—the reporter turned away, wishing the crew a good night. He strode rapidly to his room at the International Hotel. Passing through the lobby, he saw a letter in his box and reached up to take it in hand, continuing on up the staircase to his room on the second floor. There, wearily, yet with usual aplomb and discipline he sat down at his table, lit his candle by a flint and wrote his story about lamplighters in Calico. Finishing with his story, he turned to open his letter. It was from his fiancee. The missive was brief. She had heard from a man, the brother of a friend, that children had come to Calico and that the schoolhouse was completed. The town would need a teacher. She was determined to move to Calico where she could be with her sweetheart and perhaps apply for a teaching job no matter how few the number of children, or their ages. He fell asleeps across his bed, thinking that it was too late for him to stop her from moving to Calico, a town still wild, dangerous, and a place where any accident could kill the stranger to Calico who was unaware of its incipient and ready-made hazards for just plain living in an undeveloped and largely not yet civilized small western mining town.

*T*he little group of attendees at the marriage ceremony began to disperse, looks of dismay, sorrow, and fear on their faces. Mr. Dixon intended to compose an editorial condemning the arrest to appear in the next edition of the *Eagle*.

About noon of the same day, not ten days later, Jude Marlo Dempsey arrived in his black riding tunic, a pistol clinched about his waist against frequent highwaymen. He checked into the Adventure Hotel then rode to the Horseshoe Stables where he stabled his powerful black stallion for the duration of the trial.

Back at the hotel, the clerk handed him a note from the sheriff that informed the judge of the hearing, not a trial until all evidence was convicting, to be held in the town's only church sanctuary. The sheriff also informed Judge Dempsey that he, the sheriff, was holding the prisoner in an abandoned cabin behind the miners' boarding house and would at the appointed time for the hearing, ten the following morning, release the prisoner and escort him to the church for the proceedings to begin. The judge was pleased with this arrangement. He was the man who usually had to arrange for one.

The judge was the first to arrive. The pastor had arranged that he sit behind the communion table. The judge removed his straight-brimmed black hat and set it on one end of the table just as a few stragglers, curiosity seekers, strolled in and sat at the back of the sanctuary. Next came the Dixons, arm in arm, occupying benches at the front of the sanctuary. Pews were still on order, to arrive at any time. The judge nodded to greet the attendees, placed a portfolio of offical paper before him that detailed the case, and commenced to reading the case history of *Winslow v Harding*, a simpler case in California history of an alleged murder by a close friend.

Next to arrive was the accused himself, looking rather withdrawn, disheveled, and hungry. The Sheriff had drawn up his hearse-car at the door and stiffly walked the prisoner to the front of the sanctuary. The judge, impatient by nature and with miles yet to travel to visit Bay Area villages and towns, rapped with the gavel provided to him by the sheriff. Kate and Anna were the last to enter the sanctuary. He slowly walked to the front of the church and sat directly in front of the judge's table that read "Do this in Remembrance of Me."

The judge rapped again then with a grim visage that had not changed since he entered the church.

He asked, "Will the prisoner please stand."

Duval stood.

"You have been charged with the murder of a man named SBponilfact St. John at a San Francisco hotel nightclub. How do you plead?"

"I plead not guilty, Judge."

"Then let us proceed."

"Your honor, I am waiting for a chief witness to arrive. My deputies had arranged for her, and she should be arriving anytime."

"Will delay proceedings, but meantime, I wish to ask the prisoner about the circumstances in which he found himself involved that led to an alleged flight with the deceased man. We have not yet established that it was a murder. On the face of it, perhaps so, but . . ." The judge looked o the sheriff.

"I think I hear horses outside, yer honor."

The sheriff went to the front of the church and, momentarily, led a woman in who was dressed in modest street clothes with a cap and shawl for the chilly mountain weather.

Another figure had entered with no fanfare. He was Mr. McClacken, the lawyer who had promised to look into the situation. He had done so, apparently, for he came with a smile on his face, waving an envelope before the court judge and others who looked around to see the two figures enter, the witness and the attorney for the accused.

The judge banged his gavel again.

"Are all the parties to this case present? Who speaks for the accused?"

Mr. McClacken raised his hand.

"And you, sir?"

"I'm a practicing attorney, I've newly arrived in Calico. I hope to establish a law office here, sir. And I am taking this case pro bono to help Mr. Duval there."

"Good. Are there any more persons following his case."

No one raised a hand. The judge proceeded.

"Mr. Duval has pled not guilty to the charge of murder. He is your client, Mr. McClacken. Do you stand behind this pleadling?"

"I do, your honor."

"Good. My brief contains no details. I am dependent upon any witnesses to the dispute that led to a knifing of the deceased."

"I object, your honor. The way you phrase the attack, it sounds as if my client already is condemned by a charge that remains unsubstantiated."

"Accepted," said the judge.

"Will the witness for the prosecution rise and step forward."

The witness was the bar maid serving that night in the hotels sky room. It appeared that she had witnessed the fight. She came forward and sat in the chair provided by the pastor, beside the judge's communion table.

"I understand, Ms. Winslolw. Let me ask you . . . now think carefully about this."

"Yes, sir."

"Did you actually see the point of the knife enter the body of the deceased."

"Well, not exactly so. I saw the flash of the knife."

"But did you, can you say for certain that you saw the blade enter the body of the deceased . . . from your position at his back."

"I'm almost certain, sir."

"That's all, your honor."

"Dismissed."

McClacken spoke with terse and heavy masculine tones, if not gloomy then almost threatening as he proceeded in his defense of Duval.

McClacken paused while he waited for these words to register in the minds of the court.

"Your honor I have done research, medical research, on this case. I have here"—he handed a paper to the judge—"the coroner's record of the deceased. Coroners are qualified to list their observations for the court. The coroner said that there was no sign of blood poisoning in the body of the dead a man . . . he qualified his remark with the words 'beyond what was naturally expected.' Naturally expected. Then, your honor, I went to the hospital to get the medical diagnosis of the cause of death of M. Kingson. I found the most amazing thing, your honor."

The judge leaned forward and cupped one ear.

All eyes were intent upon McClacken.

"Here, your honor is the hospital record that contains in the hand of the attending doctor the cause of death of the man who up to this point, is the alleged murder."

He paused while the judge read the document.

"What you read is the official medical opinion, sir."

The judge handed the paper back to the attorney. MClacken read from the paper.

"Cause fo death, euremic poisoning. The man died of euremila."

He waved the document paper.

"Mr. Duval did not kill . . . in fact it is doubtful that in their tangle he even stabbed the deceased with such force as to cause the point of a dirty knife to enter the man's body."

He waved the paper again.

"No, ladies and gentlemen, the dead man succumbed to euremic poisoning. His kidneys failed to function, and he died of the poisons emitted by his own body. He was a diabetic."

The judge's face fell with an expression of dumbfounded surprise. Kate's and Anna's faces beamed. She began to cry and seemed to want to run to the front of the sanctuary and embrace her new husband. The sheriff wore an expression of dumbfounded amazement, and Duval looked satisfied that justice had been done.

The judge rapped his gavel once.

"I am convinced of that man's innocence, on the basis of all faulty witness and the medical document. Case closed. I declare Dylan Duval innocent of the charge of murder. There will be no justice."

"Thank you, Pastor, for the use of your sanctuary for this judicial matter. An innocent man has been justified as being a protector of the law . . . innocent."

Duval and Anna rushed toward each other and embraced. Kate escaped in the commotion. The judge donned his black straight-brimmed hat and strode with dignity out of the church. The sheriff exited with studied identity, and the bystanders, having witnessed the declaration of the lawyer McClacken, had vanished long ago. Thus ended the hearing of Dylan Duval, now to be united with his new bride of only a few days. They vanished after the judge, who strode back to the stables to pick up his mount. Mr. Dixon invited the Duvals to their home for a little celebration. The four of them climbed into Dixon's surry, and they went off toward his cabin behind the newspaper office.

That Duval and his new bilde, supremely happy over the acquittal, shared the plan for a honeymoon at the lakes where he would enjoy fishing and she could write stories for her schoolchildren.

Duxn showed Duval his editorial on false arrest and smiled and tucked the paper into a file at his home desk. They drank wine and listened to Mr. Dixon tell stories about his first days in Calico when three murders were committed, one building caught fire, and there was trouble in the mines when a part of the mine tunnel caved in, as it had once before.

"You'll never be bored living here in Calico," said Mr. Dixon and they all laughed.